ACADEMY OF MAGIC

DRAGON'S GIFT THE VALKYRIE BOOK 2

LINSEY HALL

For Goodwin and Cheetie, with love.

CHAPTER ONE

The beast's eyes glowed, fierce and red.

I crouched lower in the bushes, peering through the leaves and praying it couldn't sense me. The creature was made of magic, not flesh and blood, so I actually had no freaking clue what it could sense. But better safe than sorry.

And hey, maybe it was like a T-Rex. If I didn't move, I'd be okay.

"How's it going?" Ana's voice whispered out of the comms charm around my neck that the Protectorate had given me for this test.

"Not a great time, Ana."

"Well, you've only got fourteen minutes left, so pick up the pace. The flag should be just beyond the portals."

She was right. If I didn't get that flag, I failed. I'd been training at the Undercover Protectorate Academy for two weeks, and I was determined not to blow my first real test. All I had to do was make it through the enchanted forest and retrieve the scrap of red cloth.

No big deal.

Except magical monsters kept jumping out at me, forcing me to use my shaky magical power.

I drew in a steady breath and called upon my gift. I was no longer using an amulet to help control my sonic boom—so this was all me. The magic thrashed around inside of me as I tried to get a grip on it.

The beast roared, great jaws opening wide to reveal gleaming white fangs. Its body was made of black smoke that smelled of sulphur and death.

I gagged.

A monster from hell.

It charged, massive claws digging up the dirt as it pounded toward me. I leapt up from behind the bush and hurled my magic, the sonic boom exploding out of me.

But the boom veered right, missing the monster entirely and blowing up a Scots pine.

Shit!

The monster was so close I could see the flickering fire in its eyes. I jumped, grabbed onto the tree branch above me, and scrambled onto the limb. Rough bark scraped at my leather pants. The creature leapt, jaws snapping right beneath my perch. I climbed onto the next branch, panting.

I clung to the tree, sweat forming on my skin. Below me, the four-legged smoke monster lunged, growling and snapping, its breath so bad that my eyes watered.

I had less than fourteen minutes to snag that flag and prove I wasn't the disaster student some people believed I was.

And I was hiding in a tree.

Right—this wasn't my greatest moment.

The Academy that trained initiates to join the Undercover Protectorate had turned out to be tougher than I'd thought. With my volatile magic, I spent most of my time training on my own, unable to join the main class.

To say that gave a girl a bit of a complex was an understatement.

Until I could get a handle on my magic, I was as likely to blow up my classmates as I was to complete whatever task I'd been assigned. I had a new power over water, but that couldn't help me if there was no water around.

This challenge would allow me to advance to the next level, but that wasn't looking good.

"What's my time?" I asked Ana.

This exercise was meant to simulate a real-life op in which I had a guide on the outside. The Protectorate solved crimes and protected the vulnerable, so this was a common scenario.

"Twelve minutes, forty-five seconds," Ana said. "You've got to kill that smoke monster, then get past the last challenge."

Shit. This was going to be tight.

I called upon my sonic boom, dredging up the last of my magic. I hurled it at the beast. It collided with its smoky hide, but the blast was so weak the monster just snarled and growled louder.

Great. Just *fabulous.*

I was supposed to complete the test using my magic, but I clearly wasn't going to manage it within the time.

And I couldn't fail. Couldn't quit. My magic might be crap, but I had other skills.

Better to break the rules and finish the job than to quit.

"You're an ugly son of a witch, you know that?" I asked.

The creature just growled, a sound like metal gears grinding together. Its fangs glinted, making me shiver.

I drew my sword from the ether and prayed, "Please work."

I leapt from the tree, my sword pointing downward. It stabbed into the smoke monster, sending a tingle of electric energy up my arms. Then the creature exploded in a blast of magic that smelled of dust and pine. It blew me onto my back.

The breath *oofed* out of me. Pain flared.

Aching, I scrambled to my feet.

Yeah. That would have been easier with magic.

Something sparkly caught my eye. I looked down at my shirt.

Silver glitter coated my front.

Damn it!

Evidence that I hadn't used magic to take out the challenge. Evidence that I might not be cut out for this at all—not the way things were going lately, anyway. The little demon of doubt clawed at my mind.

Even if I managed to retrieve the flag, this was going to be a walk of shame.

"Almost there?" Ana asked.

"Yep!" I spun, memory of the forest directing me toward the middle, where the portals were located.

I'd done several tests here over the last couple weeks—enough that I'd learned the lay of the land within this enchanted glen. Fairy lights floated amongst the gnarled old trees, lighting my way toward the portals in the center. Magic of a hundred varieties sparked on the air. This place was full of supernatural beasts —some who would help you, some who would hurt you.

I sure as heck knew which ones I liked best.

I sprinted through the forest, avoiding the roots that would trip me up.

"Seven minutes!" Ana said. "Get that flag *now*, because it'll take six minutes to get back to the checkpoint."

Shit, shit, shit.

I sprinted harder, finally catching sight of the clearing with the three portals. A flash of red caught my eye. I looked up. The flag hung high in a tree.

I could do this.

I raced into the clearing, eyes on the prize.

But something else caught my gaze.

The abandoned portal glowed with a sickly, dark light. This clearing in the forest housed three portals—one to Edinburgh, one to Magic's Bend, and a final one to the Fae realm. According to Cade—the irresistibly sexy Celtic war god whom I hadn't seen in weeks—the portal to the Fae realm had been shut hundreds of years ago.

But it looked different now. No longer the dull gray of a closed portal.

Instead, black light spread out from the portal, creeping across the ground like veins of inky oil.

I stumbled to a halt, my senses hit by the dark magic that flowed from the portal. It stank of rotten eggs and felt like spiders crawling on my skin.

I shuddered

This was *wrong.*

Even the scary smoke monster hadn't had dark magic that felt like this. It'd looked evil, but it'd been created by the Protectorate trainers, so the magic hadn't actually been dark.

But *this* magic was evil.

And it was within the walls of the castle, in the heart of the Protectorate.

Hesitant, I stepped closer, reaching with my senses to feel it out.

What the hell was happening?

The normally gray surface of the portal now gleamed like black oil. I was only twenty feet from it, and the stench was enough to make my eyes water.

My breath grew shallow as I studied it, my heart pounding.

Something pressed out of the oily surface, like a figure stretching out a sheet of black latex. It reached for me, hissing.

My heart leapt into my throat, and I stumbled backward.

Holy fates!

"Breeee Blackwood." The sibilant tones snaked through me, chilling my skin. "Come to meeee."

"What are you?" My voice shook. I stiffened, raising my sword.

"Coooome." It disappeared, sinking back into the portal, which still gleamed shiny and black.

Holy fates.

My breath heaved as I inspected the portal, careful to keep my distance.

What the hell was happening? The Undercover Protectorate was supposed to be safe. This was *not* safe.

"Bree? Where are you?" Ana's voice made me jump.

"Here." My voice wasn't as strong as it should be. I'd faced down monsters for ten years, fearlessly fighting my way across Death Valley. I'd seen the worst of the worst.

Or so I'd thought.

Because *this?* This scared me. The magic felt dark and evil. Like a nightmare that bound you in iron shackles and wouldn't let go.

"You better be headed back," Ana said. "Time's almost up."

"Right." I shook my head, completely ignored the flag, and gave the portal one last, hard look. It was still shiny and black, and the inky veins crept out from it, snaking across the ground. They extended out about five feet across the forest floor.

Oh man, this is bad.

I turned and ran, sprinting through the forest, a vision of the portal blaring in my mind. My lungs burned as I jumped over roots and dodged around trees. By the time the trees thinned at the edge of the forest, my heart felt like it would explode.

I stumbled onto the main lawn of the compound. In the center, a castle rose tall, a sprawling stone structure that looked like it was straight out of a crazy fairy tale. I had to get there, had to warn someone. Warn Cade.

He was the first person who popped to mind, even though I hadn't seen him since our disastrous kiss a couple weeks ago. As usual, I'd made a move I shouldn't have.

But he wasn't here. Jude was the closest.

Loud cheers drew my eyes away from the castle.

Ana stood with Caro, the platinum-haired water sprite-demon hybrid who was our closest friend here. Next to them stood our other friends, Ali and Haris, the Djinns. Their dark hair gleamed in the summer sunlight. They'd all come to cheer me on in my last test. Now, they clapped and hollered.

I'd made it within the time limit.

I wished I had a red flag to give them instead of the news from the forest.

Jude, the head of the Paranormal Investigative Team and the one in charge of this test, looked up from her stopwatch, her star-blue eyes sparkling against her dark skin. They swept over me.

She frowned, no doubt realizing that I didn't carry the flag.

I jogged toward them, my mind racing.

"What's wrong?" Ana demanded. Her green eyes sharpened, glinting with worry. "Something's wrong."

She knew me so well.

"There's something wrong with the forest." I leaned over, panting from my run.

"Wrong? What's wrong?" Jude's voice was razor-edged. Alert.

I liked that she immediately took me seriously.

I caught my breath and straightened. "The portal to the Fae realm—the closed one? There's something wrong with it. It looks like an oil slick. And something tried to come out of it, but couldn't manage."

"Oil slick?" Caro asked.

"Never seen that before." Ali scrubbed a hand over his face, brow wrinkling with worry.

"Come." Jude snapped into work mode. "We'll have a debriefing. I want Hedy to hear this."

She took off toward the castle, her stride long and quick. She pulled a phone from her pocket, no doubt to call Hedy. I glanced at my friends, whose creased brows and worried eyes mirrored my own feelings.

None of them looked like they had any idea, but hopefully Hedy might. She was in charge of Research and Development here at the Undercover Protectorate. In my two short weeks here, I'd gotten to know everyone a bit better, and I really liked the clever witch.

I liked everything about this place, actually. Friends, a castle, security, and safety. There was even a cool pub called the Whisky and Warlock where we'd go to celebrate the end of a test.

Instead, we had something really freaking creepy to deal with.

"So, you have no idea what you saw?" Ana asked as we strode across the wide, green lawn toward the enormous castle.

"Not a clue, but it was scary as hell."

"Nothing should be able to get in here without our permission," Caro said. "Yet the thing almost succeeded?"

"Yeah." They'd increased security on the walls ever since the break-in two weeks ago. The intruder who'd been hunting Ana and me had made it in because he'd convinced a Protectorate employee to let him past the walls, but that couldn't happen anymore with the new and improved spells.

Except *something* was going on.

"Hopefully it's just a malfunction," Haris said.

"Hopefully." But I seriously doubted it.

We reached the castle courtyard, and the large wooden doors swung open to permit us entrance.

The massive entry hall was pure chaos. The Pugs of Destruction rampaged in a wide circle, their ghostly forms bowling over two trainees carrying tall piles of books. Glittering lights floated near the ceiling as if tiny fairies had infested the castle.

"Enough!" Jude roared.

The pugs stopped, turning their black eyes toward Jude, then darted off down the hall to the left. The fairy lights stilled, then disappeared up into the stone ceiling.

"A nuisance, they are," Jude muttered as she led us up the huge sweeping staircase and down the wide hall toward her office.

The five of us were silent as we followed her into the large room. The whole place was covered in maps. Not an inch of wall showed. Even the ceiling was painted with one massive mural of the world. It smelled of old paper and spices, something Jude had said preserved the paper of her precious maps.

"You can sit," Jude said.

A huge desk sat on one side of the office with a large table on the other side. Jude went to a shelf full of rolled-up maps while the rest of us found seats at the table. Hedy breezed through the door, her long blue dress fluttering behind her as her silver and lavender hair glinted in the light. She looked like a mythical version of a fairy witch.

"What's this about a problem in the forest?" she asked.

"Bree saw something." Jude approached and rolled a map out on the table. It was sparse, with little detail. Just squiggly lines that indicated a sea and a forest and possibly some buildings, but nothing was recognizable.

Jude pinned me with her gaze. "Tell us what you saw."

I looked up from the map, meeting the curious gazes of my friends and colleagues. "A black oily substance covered the portal." I explained everything I'd seen, down to the feeling of the dark magic and the creature that had tried to come out of it. "And it told me to come to it. It called to me."

"Called to you?" Jude frowned.

"Yeah." I swallowed hard. "By name."

Hedy leaned back in her chair, face creased. "That's unheard of. No one has used that portal in centuries, ever since the Fae closed it."

Jude pointed to the map. "For hundreds of years, we had access to the Fae land beyond the portal, though it's not well mapped. We could enter, and a guide would escort us. They said it was too dangerous to wander unattended."

"Then, one day, the portal was closed," Hedy said.

Ana leaned forward. "Why?"

"We have no idea," Jude said. "The records are sparse, but we don't think anyone ever knew."

"You couldn't force the portal open to find out why they closed it?" I knew the the portals into the Protectorate were locked. Had the Fae done the same?

"There is magic that could force it open," Hedy said. "A key. But we don't have it."

"It wouldn't matter if we did," Jude said. "We signed a treaty with the Fae. That portal was invitation only. Once it closed, they rescinded the invitation. To force it open would invite war."

"So if we need to go in and investigate, it could be a problem," I said.

"If it comes to that, yes," Jude said. "But if that portal is a true threat, we may need to go in anyway."

Hedy stood. "But I'd like to go check the magic for myself. This can't be good. Depending upon what we find, we'll alert the other heads of the department and decide what to do."

I nodded, liking that plan, and stood to join her.

There was no single boss of the Undercover Protectorate, as I'd learned. Caro had given Ana and me a complete rundown of operations. Arach, the dragon spirit, was the closest thing to one, but she only showed up in case of emergency. Instead, the five leaders of the different divisions made decisions as a group.

"I don't like this," Caro muttered, her sea-colored eyes dark with worry.

She wasn't the only one. The stress of the other Protectorate members hung heavy in the air. This kind of thing was clearly unusual. Their stronghold was never breached...and this was the second attempt in two weeks.

It didn't take us long to return to the forest. Ana, Caro, Ali, Haris, and I hurried along behind Jude and Hedy. The silence was tense, with even the forest animals keeping quiet. We'd had to make a stop at Hedy's workshop to gather some of her tools, and by the time we were back in the forest, my nerves were frayed.

Would the creepy figure try to come out of the portal again? To speak to me?

"It really talked to you?" Ana whispered.

"Yeah." And fates, I hoped it talked to someone else next time.

As we followed the path between the gnarled old trees, the fairy lights seemed to sparkle brighter, darting around.

"Fairy lights are anxious," Caro said.

"Something feels very wrong," Haris murmured. He rubbed his sweatshirt-clad arms and looked around nervously.

"Seconded," Ali said.

I'd never seen the guys go anywhere without tossing a ball between them or kicking their hacky sack as they walked. But now, they were as alert as if we were going into battle. Bodies tense and magic thrumming on the air. Their forms flickered in and out of existence, as if they were holding their invisibility close, ready to deploy it.

Seeing the powerful Djinn nervous ratcheted up my own sense of doom.

"We're nearly there," Jude said.

The rotten egg stink was starting to hit me, making my eyes water. "You guys smell that?"

They all sniffed, their noses wrinkling.

"A light smell of something off?" Hedy asked from up ahead on the path.

"A light smell?" I shook my head. "No way. Really strong, like rotten eggs."

"It may be getting stronger," Jude said.

She didn't sound convinced. They didn't smell it as strongly as I did.

I hurried along the path, closing the gap between me and Jude and Hedy, who led the group. We were near the clearing, close enough that I could see the black gleam of the polluted portal.

I pointed. "There, see?"

Were the black veins of dark magic even farther out now? Spreading?

We approached, stopping about twenty feet away. The portal gleamed an oily black, but the creature wasn't there.

"It looks darker," Hedy said. "The gray is nearly black?"

"Nearly?" I looked at her, shocked. "It's black as an oil spill. And the smell."

I nearly gagged just standing here.

"It's stronger now, yes." Jude's nose wrinkled. "It could be dark magic. It's quite rank."

"It's definitely dark." I turned to Ana. "You see it, right?"

A doubtful expression wrinkled her brow. "I see what they see. Dark gray. And a bit of a smell. But nothing like what you describe."

I looked at the others, confusion clouding my mind. Caro looked like she *wanted* to see it, but she didn't. Neither did Ali and Haris.

"We're not saying you're wrong," Caro said. "Just that you may be capable of seeing something we're not."

Ah, hell. If my newly developing powers involved seeing horrible dark magic that talked to me like a creepy stalker, that was *not* good.

"I'm going to test it," Hedy said. "We take all threats seriously, especially since the break-in two weeks ago."

"Is the creature here now? The one that spoke to you?" Jude's hand hovered near the long dagger at her waist. She might not see it, but she *did* believe me. Thank fates.

"No. It only appeared briefly, then disappeared."

Jude turned to Hedy, who was digging around in the big bag she'd brought along. "How long will this take you?"

"An hour or two." She pulled out her long wand. "The magic is faint. It'll take a while to identify what is happening."

Jude nodded. "You do that. When you're done, we'll convene the council." Jude looked at me and Ana. "And don't the two of you have training to be at?"

My mouth dropped open. "What about *this*?"

"Hedy has it under control. But you are still trainees. And today is the day that tutors are assigned." Her gaze dropped to my shirt, which I only now realized was covered in glitter. "And you, Bree, clearly need your tutor."

My cheeks burned at the same time a groan of frustration nearly escaped me. I choked it back.

When Ana and I had signed up for this gig, Caro had warned us that training would be a bitch.

And boy, had she been right.

I'd spent all morning fighting monsters in the forest, but that still left time for training in the afternoon. With a tutor.

Which I was *so* not going to like.

I was starting to think maybe I wasn't made of the right stuff, after all. I was a badass out in the desert, but those conditions were perfect for me. This place made me question myself in ways I never had.

"We've brought in a specialist to help you with your specific powers," Jude said, "since it's the sonic boom that is giving you the most trouble, Bree. And Ana, there will be one for your power as well."

She was right. My sonic boom—the magic I'd relied on for so long—was going totally haywire. A couple weeks ago, I'd developed a power over water that was much easier to control. Why I was having trouble with the sonic boom was anyone's guess. But I needed to learn to control it if I was going to find a place here.

I nodded. "Will you tell me what you find here?"

A tiny smile tugged at the corner of Jude's lips. "When you're done training." Her gaze fell on the rest of them. "Don't you all have something to be doing? Cases to solve?"

Caro, Ali, and Haris all jumped, then turned and hightailed it through the woods.

Ana and I followed them, sticking close together on the forest path. She was training just as hard as I was, but her goal was to expand her protective shield magic and to learn long-range weapons.

We were settling in pretty nicely at the Protectorate, even though it was totally different than our old life back in Death Valley Junction. Our days were full of training and our nights full of hanging out with Caro, Ali, and Haris—sometimes at the Whisky and Warlock in Edinburgh and other nights in our apartments.

So far, we liked it. A lot.

But if we didn't pass our tests—which were more of the fighting variety than the #2 pencil variety—we wouldn't get to join. So we worked our butts off.

I hadn't seen Cade, which was both a blessing and a curse, but all in all, everything had been going pretty smooth until now.

"Are you doing all right?" Ana asked.

"Yeah. Freaked out, but I'll be fine." I glanced at her. "You really didn't see the black oil slick over the portal?"

"No. Just that it looked a little different."

Damn. Worry nagged me as we walked in silence across the lawn.

We approached the main door of the castle, which loomed overhead, towers reaching for the sky. Mullioned windows glittered in the sunlight, and statues of gargoyles peered down at us. The massive wooden doors swung open, and we entered, hesitating once we reached the middle of the foyer.

"I think we're supposed to meet in the training room on the second level," Ana said. "Do you know who your new trainer is?"

"No. Schedule didn't say." At the beginning of each week, we received a list of training and tests we'd have to pass. This one had included a meeting on the second floor where we each hooked up with a trainer.

"Do you think they'll be able to help with your sonic boom?" Her gaze dropped to my shirt, where the glitter of shame still sparkled.

"I sure hope so." Because my magic was just as bonkers as ever, despite all the work I'd done here to improve. I could manipulate water when it was nearby, but controlling my sonic boom was nearly impossible. I lowered my voice so only she could hear. "If our magic is supposed to be from dragons, as Arach and our mother said, shouldn't I have more control? Be *better* than this?"

A sad expression crossed Ana's face, and she shrugged. "I have no idea." She looked at her hands, as if inspecting them for the magic she usually threw out. "I sure as heck don't feel like I have the magic of dragons. All I can do is create a protective shield."

I squeezed her shoulder. Ana loathed the fact she had defensive magic in an offensive world. "At least you have control of it."

"For now. But I'll go through my change, too. And then I'll be in your spot."

"We'll get through it. Together." My gaze caught on a man who walked into the foyer behind Ana. He carried a massive stack of books. An idea flared. I met Ana's gaze. "There's got to be an enormous library here. What do you say we check it out after training? See if we can figure out anything about our magic."

She grinned. "I like how you think."

"We're here, aren't we? They've got more resources that we could never imagine. Let's use them."

She held up her fist for a bump. I bopped it with my own and grinned.

"Great idea, nerd," she said.

"Love you, double-nerd. Now, let's go." I saluted, then turned and took the left sweeping staircase and ran up two at a time, Ana at my side.

We raced by an older man who tutted at us.

"Sorry," I muttered, then turned left, making my way down the wide stone corridor.

Once again, I was struck by the history and grandeur of the place. A few people passed me, but only two shot me suspicious looks. Not bad. Two was an improvement.

We found the second story training room and stopped at the door. I glanced at Ana and winked, then pushed it open to reveal a large room with a vaulted ceiling and large windows at the end.

Three other trainees—two guys and one girl, turned to look at us—suspicion in their gazes. They'd entered the Academy shortly before us—it was a bit like a magical version of that FBI academy. But we hadn't mixed with them much, given that my weird powers kept me away from most of the class.

"Hey, Ana," the girl said, looking through me.

I scowled. Not like I was going to throw my sonic boom at her and blow her up.

"Hey, Lacey," Ana said.

My gaze caught on a group of five figures at the far end of the room, silhouetted against the bright glass. They stood in a circle speaking, but one stood out from the others.

He looked familiar—at least his size. Then his power hit me. The scent of a storm at sea, the sound of clashing swords and the taste of fresh apples.

My stomach dropped as heat curled low inside me. My skin prickled with awareness, and a light sense of panic suffused my mind.

The five figures disbanded and approached. As they neared, I got a feel for each of their signatures, but it was Cade's who stood out to me.

Cade. The sexy Celtic war god.

CHAPTER TWO

Shit, shit, shit. The last time I'd seen Cade, I'd kissed him smack on the mouth. It'd been *amazing*. Award-worthy.

And then excruciatingly embarrassing. Like any rational person would do, he'd told me it couldn't happen again because we both worked for the Protectorate. A conflict of interest.

The worst thing was…he had a point. Workplaces and flirting were a recipe for awkwardness, at best, and lawsuits, at worst.

Heat burned my cheeks. As much as I still wanted him—and *boy* did I—all I could remember was the searing embarrassment.

But there was *no* way he was going to be my trainer. This had to be a mistake. My head buzzed as one of the other trainers stepped forward, a tall woman with long, blonde hair. She cleared her throat, then began to give a lecture about learning from a more advanced member of the Protectorate. I barely processed a word she said.

Then the trainers split up, each heading toward one of the trainees.

Of course, Cade stopped in front of me. We were a good fifteen feet from any of the other trainees, who'd gone off toward the side of the room. It felt like they were miles away. All I could see was Cade—broad-shouldered, quick-witted, handsome as the devil Cade.

"You?" I demanded.

"Me." His low voice, coated in that sexy Scottish accent, wrapped around me.

"I thought you only took the most dangerous jobs," I said.

"Aye." He pointed at me. "And *you* are the most dangerous job."

I scoffed. "Hardly."

"You can blow up a house with your magic only partially charged. And you haven't gained any more control over that magic in the two weeks you've been here. You're a walking time bomb." He towered over me. His shoulders were broad enough to block out the light from the windows, and his jawline could cut glass.

My breath shortened as I leaned my head back to make sure my glare landed solidly on him and tried not to focus on his heady scent. It was so good that it distracted me, and I couldn't afford that. But I'd forgotten how tall he was. At least six and a half feet if he was an inch.

My mind went straight toward our kiss. The feel of his lips, the scent of his skin. It made my head swim.

I shook it.

Get it together.

To get my mind out of the gutter, I went through the sneaky moves I'd use to take him out, a habit I'd gotten into early in life. Right now, it was better than thinking about kissing him. And a dude as big as Cade would require some serious sneakery to take down.

"You're thinking about how you'd take me out, aren't you?" He grinned.

"Uh, no."

He just grinned wider, becoming even more devastatingly attractive.

"Fine. Yes, I was. But how'd you know?"

"Great minds think alike."

"Oh, you're thinking about how you'd take me out?" *Crap!* I slapped a hand over my mouth as heat blazed into my cheeks. "And by that, I meant like a wrestling move. To take me *out* out. Like in a fight. Not like, in the other way."

Holy fates, I need to be put in an insane asylum. Somewhere I'd never see humans again and be able to open my mouth. He'd *just* called me a conflict of interest. Now I was talking about dates?

The corners of his full lips pulled up in a smile and he nodded. "Of course. A wrestling move. Absolutely nothing else."

"Why you?" I asked. "Couldn't someone else train me?"

"I'm the only one who can withstand your sonic boom. If it goes awry and hits me, I'll be fine."

Right. Shit. Of course.

Back in Death Valley, I'd hit him with a sonic boom meant to pulverize his insides. He hadn't even wobbled on his feet.

I couldn't fight that logic.

"Fine." I cracked my knuckles. "Let's get this party started. What do I do first, Teach?"

"Let's take it outside."

"Fair enough." I didn't want to blow up my new home. Especially not a castle this cool.

"This way." He turned and strode toward the door.

I followed him out of the castle, my eyes constantly darting toward him.

"We'll go over there." He pointed to a spot near the enchanted forest. "The magic of the forest might help give you some control."

"Really?" I'd never heard of anything like that before.

"That's where the dragons' magic is the strongest. It's the place they originally enchanted with their magic."

"Is that why the Fae built their portal there?" I asked, wondering if I should mention the issue with the portal. But

Hedy and Jude had it under control. And if I didn't like what they told me about it, maybe I'd mention it.

I hoped they'd believe that it was a big deal. Because if they didn't….I'd have to take matters into my own hands. Something was clearly wrong, and I couldn't just ignore it.

"It's the reason they were able to build the portal there, aye," Cade said. "Wait here a moment." He jogged toward the forest and disappeared inside, returning after a few moments with an armful of large, dead branches.

His expression upon leaving the forest was slightly off—wrinkled brow, worried eyes.

"What is it?" I asked, wondering if he felt it too.

I couldn't be crazy. I'd really seen that black oil slick and heard the monster that had tried to escape.

"Forest feels off," he said.

I was about to open my mouth to explain, but he shook his head. "Could just be me. Years of war have made me wary. But you need to train."

He turned away from me to set the sticks up in a semicircle, each about thirty meters from the other. He dusted off his hands and looked at me. "Targets."

"All right." I rubbed my sweating palms against my jeans. I'd focus on this for an hour, give Hedy and Jude long enough to figure out the problem in the forest, then I'd maybe mention it to Cade.

Everyone was right, anyway. I really needed to get a handle on my magic. The amulet Cade had given me before to help me control my magic had been a temporary stopgap. *I* needed to be the one driving this car.

"So, you just want me to blast one?" I asked.

"It's a start."

"Yep." One that I wasn't feeling super great about. But I tried, because what else was I going to do?

I sucked in a deep breath and called upon my magic. As usual, it zipped around my chest like a lightning bug on speed. Finally, I caught it, mentally gathering it up and hurling it outward.

The sonic boom plowed into the ground about ten meters to the left of the tree branch.

I winced.

I was *bad.*

"Again." Cade crossed his arms over his chest.

"Okay." I sucked in another deep breath and tried again.

Missed.

Frustration welled in my chest, a hard knot.

"Has it always been like this?" Cade asked.

"Getting worse lately."

"All right. Try again. This time, clear your mind."

I did as he said, but this time, the sonic boom that plowed out of me was so large it destroyed all the branches and created a crater in the lawn.

I gasped and stumbled backward. "Crap!"

Cade frowned. "Did you mean for it to be that big?"

"No!" I shook my hands as if I could force the frustration out of me. "It just does that sometimes."

"Wild card."

"Yeah." I didn't make a habit of getting down on myself, but damned if it wasn't hard when I was faced with the reality of what my magic was becoming.

What *I* was becoming.

"But you're not terrible with a sword, or you'd be dead."

"I'm excellent with a sword."

His face creased with doubt. "You've got skinny arms. You were good in Oregon and Venice, but you weren't fighting a real warrior."

"Like you?"

"Exactly." He drew a sword from the ether, a long blade that looked wickedly sharp. "Try me."

"Oh, so we're doing this now, are we?" Excitement thrummed

21

in my chest. I drew my own sword, which was so much lighter and smaller than his.

He approached, sword raised.

Holy shit, this was happening. I grinned. *This* was something I could do. We circled each other, probably looking ridiculous. Anybody my size with a lick of sense wouldn't go up against a god of war who was six and a half feet tall.

Fortunately, I had more skill than sense.

He lunged first, and I darted left and blocked with my blade. The sheer strength of his blow bent my arm backward, and I barely slipped away in time.

The next strike was even harder, making my arm go almost numb. I dodged, then pretended to stumble.

He didn't fall for it, backing up instead of pouncing as I'd hoped.

"Clever," I said.

"Always."

I went on the offensive, charging and swiping out with my blade. Before his could block it, I sliced down, toward his legs. He danced back, sparing himself a slice by mere millimeters.

His appraising eyes met mine. "Nice."

"Like I said…excellent. Even against a god of war." I lunged again, this time trying a move that required more speed than strength.

Unfortunately, he was fast, too. He knocked my blade aside with his and reached out with his free arm, grabbing me around the waist and swinging me to the ground.

"Ooof!" Pain flared in my back as I scrambled upright, barely keeping a grip on my sword. I danced back from him. "Are you tempering your strength?"

"How could you tell?"

"My bones aren't broken."

He grinned. "Fair assessment."

"Well, don't pull any punches with your sword work. When I beat you, I want it to be real."

"Beat me?" He laughed.

"What? God of war doesn't mean god of swords."

"We'll see."

"Hmmm, we will." We went round and round like that, striking and defending, parrying and blocking. I landed a couple light blows, but he was too fast to ever take a real hit.

Same for me. Though there were a few moments that made me feel like I might lose a limb, I dodged them by a hair.

Sweat pearled at my temples and my mind was laser focused.

I did better this time, meeting him evenly, as long as he used his sword and not his strength.

Finally, he stepped back, hands raised. "A draw."

Man, he looked good when he was fighting. I grinned, propping my sword blade on my shoulder. "You're too scared to keep going. You think I'm going to beat you."

"No. But I can see when I'm evenly matched. You're good."

"I know I'm good." I tapped my chin. "Actually, I remember saying I was excellent."

"I wouldn't disagree."

"Good." I went to point my sword at him and crow a little more—had to take the victories where I could get them—then it dawned on me. I lowered my sword. "Heyyy."

"Aye?"

"Did you do that to get my confidence up? Pick something I'm good at?"

"Are you accusing me of pulling my punches?"

"Not with your sword, no. You're sweating. And you were really trying there. I tied you fair and square. All I'm saying is that you might have had an ulterior motive. My magic may be a disaster, but no one has ever doubted I'm a badass with my blade. So you weren't testing my blade."

"Fine, I may have been—" His eyes widened on something behind me.

I whirled, sword raised. The forest was cast in shadow from the setting sun. Something flashed out of the corner of my vision. Cade's arm?

A massive beast hurtled out of the forest, thundering toward us on giant hooves. The monster was the size of a truck, a great skeletal boar with pieces of tattered flesh and muscle hanging from its bones. Its head was huge, with giant fangs and two long tusks. Eyes of flame blazed at us.

A zombie boar? Or a hellbeast?

Was it the thing from the portal?

My heart thundered in my chest as the monster charged us, his hoofbeats shaking the ground beneath my feet. The creature reeked of death and evil.

Joy sang through me, tinged strongly with fear. I felt like I was back on top of the buggy, fighting monsters in Death Valley.

This was what I loved. What I lived for. Where I felt most comfortable. I might have been scared out of my pants, but it was my usual.

I sucked in a deep breath, shoved the fear aside, and called upon my magic, grabbing hold of it and hurling it outward. The sonic boom exploded, shooting through the air and plowing into the beast, scattering its bones like candy flying out of a gruesome piñata.

Then the bones disappeared into thin air.

The boar—all evidence of it—was gone.

What the heck?

Understanding dawned. It hadn't been the monster from the portal. My heart thundered, from fear and joy and stress all at once.

I turned on Cade, noting the smile on his face. A sexy smile, that bastard.

I pointed at him. "You did that."

"What?" He held up his hands, trying to look innocent.

"You've never looked innocent a day in your life, so don't even try."

He grinned.

"You got my confidence up with the sword fight, then used magic to create the boar."

"I can't create boars."

"No, but you could throw something that could create a boar. Some kind of fancy spell made by Hedy, maybe?"

His eyes flickered.

I pointed at him. "Gotcha. That's what you did."

"And you blasted it away on the first shot."

"I do best under pressure. When the threat is real." I shrugged. "Or feels real, at least."

"Which is what I suspected. Well done, Bree. Your magic might be going haywire, but we can count on you in a dangerous situation."

I returned my sword to the ether. "Of course you can. My whole life has been a dangerous situation."

"Aye. It's what made you strong."

Well, I didn't hate the sound of that.

My gaze darted toward the forest, the memory of the portal distracting me from the compliment. Sure, it was Jude and Hedy's job to figure it out. Not my place. I was a trainee, after all.

Ha. As if that would stop me.

I'd never been very good at following rules, after all. And this was important. I knew it was.

"Cade, there's something I have to tell you."

His gaze changed, turning almost wary.

Shit. He thought I was going to talk about *us*. There was no us. And I wasn't dumb enough to force the issue. I had to have my pride, after all. "There's a problem in the forest. A portal. I saw it when—"

"Bree! Cade!" The shout cut me off.

I turned, spotting Jude, Hedy, and the librarian coming out of the forest.

Potts, I thought he was called. I'd only met the stooped old man once, and he'd been a grouch.

"That's odd. Potts doesn't leave his library unless forced." Cade turned to me. "Are you talking about one of the portals in the forest? Is that where they are coming from?"

"Yes. Maybe they should tell you."

The three of them hurried toward us, Potts moving much faster than I'd have expected him to. He looked to be about a hundred and fifty if he was a day. Worry creased Hedy's brow, and her face was slightly blackened by silver dust. Magic gone awry? Jude's expression was stern, as usual. Ready to deal with the problem, whatever it was.

They stopped in front of us.

Jude's gaze landed on me. "The portal is a problem, Bree. Good job spotting it."

"Thanks."

"What's going on?" Cade asked.

I was bouncing on my feet, dying to know what the heck was happening in the forest.

It was bad. I knew it like I knew I liked pink cocktails.

Jude nodded and explained the problem I'd found. "Hedy just finished her tests. She revealed the dark curse on the portal—the one that you could see, Bree."

"There is something slowly leaching out of the portal. A spell." Hedy's gaze turned to me. "But you said that a creature tried to climb out? And it spoke to you?"

"Yes. It told me to come to it. It probably would have tried to get to me, but the portal stretched, holding it in."

"This has never happened before." Cade's brow furrowed. "We need to perform recon."

"Can't you just destroy the portal to keep the curse from coming through?" I asked.

"Unfortunately, no," Hedy said. "It is far too ancient, which means the magic is too strong."

Damn.

"Recon is our best option." Jude nodded. "Potts confirmed that no one has used that portal in over three hundred years."

"The records don't lie." Potts's voice was whispery with age. He looked like he should smell of dust rather than evergreen.

"I have a map," Jude said. "It's old and incomplete, but you can use it to start your recon."

"Good," Cade said. "I can start right away."

Jude pointed to me. "Bree as well."

Potts huffed. "I still say she's too young! Untrained."

"That may be true," Jude said. "But she's the only one who has seen the monster. Felt its magic. It called to her."

"I can track it," I said. "Or at least identify it. The magic was unique. That'll help."

Potts made some grousing noises, clearly unable to contain himself. "But she's only completed her first tests. She has so many more to finish! She's unproven."

While I was annoyed, he did have a point.

"We can count on her in true danger," Cade said. "I vouch for Bree."

My cheeks—and my heart—warmed at his words.

"As do I," Jude said. "I know it's unusual to send a trainee on an important job like this, but Bree is unusually talented. This can count as one of her tests."

Heck yeah. One less timed fight in the forest was fine with me. I hated the false danger—give me the real thing any day.

"Thank you," I said. "I won't let you down."

I hoped.

Was I cut out for this? I didn't know, but I was going to try. I *had* to try. The monster who'd called my name made that clear.

"See that you don't," Jude said. "And you'll have to be careful. Remember what I said about the Fae. With the portal locked, we are no longer invited there. This threat may be coming from them, or from someone else. But be quick on your toes."

"Don't piss them off and start a war, you mean."

"Exactly."

"And hurry. That magic is spreading." Hedy's gaze was dark with worry. "And it's the darkest we've ever seen. This is a serious problem."

"So, we need to go into the portal to find where the spell is coming from," I said. "And stop it."

And figure out why the heck it said my name.

That was freaky.

"Exactly," Jude said. "But to get through the portal, you need to make sure the dark magic doesn't cling to you. It would coat you like oil, and there's no telling what it could do to you."

"I have a contact in Edinburgh who can help." Hedy handed me a glass vial full of the oily black substance that glazed the portal. It prickled against my palm. "She's an Eclektica. A jack-of-all-trades who deals in spells. She can sell you something that will make you immune to the curse so that you can pass through unharmed. She'll also give you a key to help you unlock the portal. It's been closed so long that it will take special magic to open it."

"We'll go find her right now," Cade said.

"Go to the Whisky and Warlock," Hedy said. "Tell Sophie at the bar that you need to see Tabitha. She'll take you where you need to go."

"Thank you for this chance," I said. "I'll find out what's going wrong."

"We hope you will," Jude said.

Hedy's gaze turned concerned. "In fact, we're counting on it."

So was I.

CHAPTER THREE

We had to return to the woods in order to get to Edinburgh. The poisoned portal gleamed with black oil, the stench filling the clearing as we approached the portal that led to the Scottish capital.

It glowed blue and bright, welcoming.

"At least the Fae portal hasn't poisoned this one," I said.

The corner of Cade's mouth tipped up. "I couldn't agree more. This is my way home."

"You live in the city, right?"

"Aye." He stepped up to the portal, then glanced at me. "Ready?"

"Always."

He grinned, then stepped through. I followed, letting the ether suck me in. It pulled me through space, making my head spin, then spat me out onto the sidewalk of a bustling city street.

It was a wild ride every time I used this portal, but it was beyond cool that the Protectorate's castle was just a step away from a big city.

All around, the Grassmarket bustled with life. Supernaturals of every variety hurried down the sidewalks on either side of the road, popping into pubs and restaurants and shops.

"I really like it here," I said.

"Different than Death Valley Junction?" Cade asked.

"*So* different."

While there was magic in Death Valley Junction, it didn't feel half as awesome as this place. The Grassmarket was the Supernaturals-only section of Edinburgh, and it bustled with magical species of all varieties. Shop windows revealed shelves of potions, magical books, trinkets, and even enchanted foods.

But my favorite part of Edinburgh was the Whisky and Warlock, the pub I occasionally visited in the evenings with Ana, Caro, Ali, and Haris. A long day of tests and training deserved the pinkest cocktail in the bar. Fortunately, Sophie, the bartender, was a pro. I hadn't had the same drink twice, and every one had been amazing.

I turned, heading down the street toward my new hangout. The sun was heading toward the horizon, sending a golden glow over the cobbled street. It warmed the faces of the historic buildings, lending them an even more magical air.

We ducked under the low doorway and into the old pub. A fat black cat named Kitty sat on a chair in front of the crackling fire, and she welcomed us with a meow. I turned left into the little room with the bar where Sophie worked. The pub was like a maze, rooms and halls and nooks and crannies. But this was our room, where the Protectorate hung out.

Sophie turned, a grin spreading across her face. Today, her dark hair was pulled up, and her T-shirt read *Thank fates Festival is over.*

"Bree! Not your usual time." Her gaze went to Cade. "And you haven't been here in ages."

Probably not since I'd seen him here last. My cheeks burned. Had my impromptu kiss kept him away because he'd known he'd see me here?

With my luck, that was the case.

"Then it's about time," Cade said.

I leaned against the bar. "Hey, Sophie. We need to see Tabitha, if you don't mind."

Sophie's eyebrows jumped up. "Tabitha? Something wrong?"

"Hopefully not," I said.

"Well, I'll ring her. It'll take her a little while to get here. What will you have?"

It was only polite to buy something if we took up real estate on the bar stools. "Something low alcohol. Pink, preferably."

"No problem. One Dirty Shirley coming right up."

"Pint of Tennent's," Cade said.

Sophie nodded and turned, going toward the phone.

"Not whisky?" I asked. It was what he'd ordered last time.

"Don't want the hard stuff before a job."

I grinned, liking the responsible answer. I'd seen too many drunken losers in Death Valley Junction.

Sophie called Tabitha from the big black phone on the wall, then set about making our drinks. I leaned on the bar, tried to ignore the prickles of awareness at Cade's proximity, and checked out the crowd. It was sparse at the moment, just a small crowd of Protectorate members sitting in the corner, in front of a hearth filled with glowing orange fire and a big black cauldron.

The people looked familiar, but I hadn't met them.

They didn't shy away from shooting me suspicious glances, however.

Ugh, being the new girl.

I looked away as Sophie approached, our drinks in hand. "One pint of Tennent's and a Dirty Shirley!"

"Thanks." I took mine and sipped.

Yum.

Tasted sweet and bright. Cherry, maybe.

I nodded toward the Protectorate members in the corner. "What's their problem?"

Cade lowered his beer and glanced over at them. He frowned. "They're old guard. Been with the Protectorate for years. They're usually suspicious of new recruits."

"Me in particular, huh?"

The blonde woman on the left was shooting me the hairy eyeball.

"If I had to guess, it's that you don't train with the others," he said. "They can't get their usual gossip on you, so they're doubly wary."

Hmmm. I might have made good friends in Caro, Ali, and Haris, but it seemed I had a few more folks to win over.

The question was if I'd ever bother.

"Don't let them trouble you," he said. "You'll earn your place here."

My heart warmed. He said it to be nice, but it sounded genuine. And it felt good. "Thanks." I turned toward him. "Have you ever met Tabitha?"

"Twice. She'll be taking us to The Vaults."

"What's that?"

"There are a series of ancient tunnels built under Edinburgh. A section of them are used by the dark magic practitioners. But you need an escort to gain entrance."

Ooooh, creepy. I liked it.

A voice sounded from behind us. "Cade, Cade, Cade. Long time no see."

I turned to see a woman step through the doorway.

Her hair gleamed black and sleek, and she wore a black leather jacket over a red and blue kilt. Combat boots completed the ensemble.

"Tabitha." Cade grinned. "Glad you could meet us."

She shrugged. "It's my job, isn't it?"

"That it is," Cade said.

I finished the last sip of my Dirty Shirley and waved. "I'm Bree."

"Good to meet you." Tabitha hiked a thumb toward the exit. "You ready to get a move on?"

We nodded and followed her out onto the street, which was now shrouded in dusk.

This close, I could smell Tabitha's magic—the scent of the beach and the feel of warm sun on my skin. Her magic was strong, but strange.

"What do you do, Tabitha?" I asked as she led us down the cobblestone sidewalk toward the cliff, upon which perched the hulking Edinburgh castle.

"I'm a runner. And a bouncer—sort of. Some people have passes to get into The Vaults, others don't. If you don't, you come to me."

We passed a Fae with her blue wings glittering in the light of the street lamps, and dodged around a couple of demons who probably shouldn't be wandering free.

But hey, I wasn't the cops. And not all demons were bad, so who was I to say?

The historic buildings rose tall on either side, their windows revealing all kinds of magical goodies. Most were closing up as the people began to choose restaurants and bars over shopping.

We were about twenty yards from where the street dead-ended into the castle cliff when Tabitha stopped abruptly.

"Hold on," she murmured.

We stopped, both stiffening. I hated being so aware of Cade, but it did help in situations like this.

Tabitha shifted toward the building, letting people pass us on the sidewalk. We followed, pressing close to the brick wall.

"What is it?" I asked.

"Up ahead. See those four guys?" Tabitha jerked her chin toward a group of men who were loitering on the sidewalk, leaning against the brick wall and drinking from flasks.

"Order members," I murmured. I hadn't seen many of them in Death Valley Junction, but my mother had taught me to recognize them by their perfect posture, buzzed hair, and their pressed clothes—no matter what they wore. Their sweatpants would be pressed when they went to the gym.

With our unknown magic, it'd been important to stay under the radar. *Way* under the radar.

Since the Order didn't approve of Unknowns such as ourselves, learning to identify them had been a survival tactic.

"Bingo," Tabitha said. "Order, all day long."

"They're on a stakeout," Cade said.

"Trying to blend in, but failing." I eyed the only one with long hair. A wig—definitely. All of their clothes were meant to look casual and sloppy, but I could see where they'd shaken out the creases. Just the faintest lines. And their posture was too good. If there'd been only one, I might not have noticed. But four?

Yeah, definitely Order members on a stakeout.

"But what are they staking out?" I asked.

"The entrance to The Vaults. It's right there, at the base of the castle." Tabitha cursed low under her breath. "I'd heard rumors that the Order was sniffing around. Not everyone uses dark magic in The Vaults, but most do."

The Order of the Magica tended to disapprove of dark magic, which I couldn't blame them for. More often than not, it was used for unsavory purposes.

But we currently needed some of that dark magic. Though the Order and the Protectorate would pretty much always be on the same side, Caro had explained that the Order's hard-on for rules and regulations slowed down the Protectorate, who always took the difficult jobs the government didn't want. Helping the little guys, solving the unknown cases, protecting the disenfranchised. That kind of thing.

"Can we sneak past?" I asked.

"No. But I've got something better." Tabitha darted into an alley on our right. "Come on."

We followed her through the quiet, winding alley.

Tabitha whispered back over her shoulder, "We'll sneak up on them from behind. Tie them up, and I'll alter their memories."

"You're a mind mage?" I asked.

Tabitha waggled her fingers. "The best. It's why I do this job. I help newbs sneak into The Vaults—not everyone knows how to be careful."

We turned down an alley that spit out onto the street where the Order members stood. I could see the shoulders of one man who stood closest to the alley entrance.

"We need to lure them in," Tabitha said. "Can't make a scene on the street. It's too busy."

My gaze darted around the alley. There was a trash bin positioned about twenty feet from the end of the alley.

I looked at Tabitha and Cade. "Cade, you pretend to attack Tabitha. Tabitha, you scream for help. I'll hide behind the bin and ambush them as they come to save you."

Tabitha gave a thumbs-up. "I like it. Except I'm no damsel in distress. I'll be Oscar the Grouch, you be Princess Peach."

Oscar the...? *Oh.* The *Sesame Street* character who lived in the trash bin. I had no idea who Princess Peach was, but she was obviously a damsel in distress.

"Fine," I said. "I'll be the princess."

Tabitha dug into her bag and pulled out some short lengths of rope, then handed them to us. "Tie them up once you catch them."

We took the ropes, then crept toward the trash bin to set up our scene. Tabitha crouched down and pressed herself against the wall, her nose wrinkling at the scent of rotting garbage. There was some kind of greasy puddle right under her feet.

Suddenly, I didn't mind playing the damsel so much.

I gripped the ties that Tabitha had given me in one hand and conjured my dagger in the other, then pressed my back against the wall and looked at Cade.

Tension over the coming fight rose in my chest, the usual pre-fight jitters. I made a face at Cade, sneering. "Come at me, bro."

The corner of Cade's full lips kicked up at the goofy tone in my voice. He stepped close and loomed over me, shoulders blocking out what little moonlight there was. His hands went to the bricks on either side of my face, caging me in. The ties that Tabitha had given him dangled from one hand.

Immediately, the scent of a storm at sea drowned out the gross alley stink, and his heat warmed my front. Though we weren't touching, it felt like the air between us was lit with sparks.

My pre-fight jitters vanished as I imagined the feel of every inch of him, his hard muscles pressed against me. It made my breath come short and my skin blaze.

I glanced up at him, catching the hard set of his jaw that was such a contrast with his full lips. Banked desire burned in the depths of his green eyes.

Tension crackled.

He was just as aware of me as I was of him.

And *this* was why I'd wanted to be on trash bin duty.

"Guys! Guys!" Tabitha's low hiss broke through my trance. "Get it together."

Fates, we'd just totally blacked out on a job. It'd only been for a few seconds, but gazing at each other like two sex-starved teenagers had been *bad*.

My gaze darted away from Cade's, but I could still feel every inch of him even though we didn't touch. "Yeah, yeah, we're ready."

"I'll take two," Cade murmured.

"Deal." I glanced at Tabitha. "I'll take the one you don't grab."

"Leave minimal bruising," Tabitha said. "No killing. If you can hold him till I get to him, I'll use my tricks to make him compliant."

Fine by me. Killing people was high on my No Thanks list.

Demons and monsters, no prob. People? Nope.

"On three," Cade said. He counted down.

On one, I looked toward the end of the alley and screamed, trying to give it a real hint of fear.

As expected, the Order members jumped up, then raced down the alley. Cade leaned closer, as if he were homing in on his attack, but I kept my gaze on the oncoming men.

They ran two by two.

My heart thundered as they neared. I vibrated with readiness, wanting to jump into it.

"Let her go!" one shouted.

"Bastard!" hissed another.

I almost felt bad about the sneak attack. When they were almost upon us, Cade whirled and grabbed the first two by their collars, dragging them back into the alley.

Tabitha leapt out from behind her trash bin and threw herself at one man, taking him down in pile of limbs.

I lunged for the other, using my body weight to force him onto his back. He was a stocky guy, which made my landing pretty cushy. He grunted and thrashed, swinging a fist for my face.

I dodged, pressing my blade to his throat. "Hold still!"

His palm fired up with a glow of red magic. Red liquid dripped from it, and his magic felt like acid prickling against my skin.

Ah, hell.

Whatever his magic was, I knew I wouldn't like it. I'd put money on acid or poison sweat, and neither of those sat on my list of favorite things.

I pressed the dagger slightly deeper, not enough to really cut but enough to make him know I meant business. "Come on, guy. Chill."

He was about to slam his palm against my shoulder when Tabitha lunged toward us, laying her hand over his face.

"Calm down," she whispered. "Forget the last three minutes."

He slumped immediately, jaw going slack.

"Holy fates, Tabitha." I reared back, staring at her in horror. "What the hell?"

"I'm a really strong mind mage." She darted around us and sprinted toward Cade and the others.

He'd dragged them back in the alley and wrapped his arms around both of them in a bear hug that looked like it was squeezing the breath from them. They were both conscious, but barely, their heads lolling.

Tabitha placed her hands on the men's faces, and they slumped in Cade's superhero-looking arms.

She stepped back and brushed her hands together. "Bring them over with the others."

Cade carried them over as if they weighed nothing, though each had to be over two hundred pounds. He laid them on the ground with the other two, and Tabitha bent low over them, laying her hands on their faces.

"Your recon determined that The Vaults is no longer here. It closed down two years ago. Now, sleep." She moved on and did the last two Order members, then stood and turned toward us. "Ready?"

I saluted. "Anything you say, boss, as long as you don't zap my memory."

She smiled and shook her head. "I couldn't even if I wanted to. I took a vow to use my power only for good."

"Like a superhero?" Maybe superheroes were on my mind after seeing Cade's arms in action.

"Exactly. My gift won't make people do anything crazy, but it can do little stuff like that. And only if it won't permanently harm someone." She shrugged. "It's not like I told them to forget their wives or anything. I'm not a monster."

No, but she was definitely a badass. "Fair enough. Let's go."

We hurried out of the alley, leaving the men to their naps, and rejoined the night crowd on the sidewalks. It was emptier at this end of the street, and Tabitha led us quickly to the cliff face.

There was a long set of narrow stone stairs leading up between the buildings toward the Royal Mile, the human area of town. On the other side of that, pressed between the stairs and the cliff face, stood a narrow building.

"Come on." Tabitha waved us toward the door.

We followed her through the entry, into a cluttered old bookstore. The lights were dim, and every volume was bound in leather. Piles of books towered toward the ceiling, leaving a path toward the back.

My heart leapt at the sight of all the old tomes. I'd never had much time to read in Death Valley, nor the money for books. And school had definitely never been a priority. Or a possibility, most of the time.

I knew I wasn't as smart as I could be. Or should be.

But these books were *awesome.*

"Why are we in a bookstore?" I asked.

"Not just a bookstore, dearie." The voice echoed through the room.

I spun in a circle, looking for the voice's owner. From the sound of her, she would be 102 if she was a day and with white hair and a flowered dress. I just knew it. The voice was *so* distinct.

"There's no one here," Tabitha said. "This is the entry to The Vaults."

"So the *house* is talking to me?" I ran my gaze over every corner and crevice I could find. There really was no one else here.

"Don't speak of me in the third person." The house *humphed.* "Ruuude!"

"Sorry! She's new." Tabitha looked at me. "Come on."

"Nice to meet you," I said.

"Likewise. Don't touch anything."

Damn.

We followed Tabitha back through the stacks of books. She dug into her pocket, pulled out a glowing golden stone, and held it up. "If you don't have one of these, the house pretends to be closed for the afternoon."

"Then the person just leaves?" I asked.

"Of course!" the house said. "Don't be ridiculous. I have control of this place."

Weird. But I didn't dare say it out loud. I didn't like horror movies, but I'd seen enough commercials advertising them to know that possessed houses always won.

Tabitha stopped at a wide wooden doorway and pressed her golden stone to the wood. Magic sparked on the air, smelling of incense carried on a fresh breeze. The door swung open.

"This way." Tabitha led us onto a dark and quiet street.

Historic-looking shops, no more than two stories tall, lined the cobblestone road that was devoid of vehicles. A few people walked along it, their figures illuminated by the golden street lamps. I studied the nearest shop, realizing it was built right into the stone mountain. It'd been carved to look like a building with a roof and everything, but it was all made of stone.

Overhead, the stars twinkled high in the night sky. But the air didn't smell as fresh as it did outside.

"This is crazy," I said.

"Isn't it?" Tabitha grinned. "We're beneath the castle. A spell makes it look like the sky is up there, but it's just rock."

An older man with white-streaked hair appeared in the doorway of the shop I'd been studying. He glared at me, his wrinkled face disapproving.

"Get along!" he huffed. "Always loitering, the new ones. Either come in and buy an enchanted pygmy toad, or get off my stoop."

An enchanted pygmy toad? From a shop that smelled of mold and old paper? No thanks. Not even if the toad was enchanted to do dishes.

"Come on, Amos," Tabitha cajoled. "Chill your ride. We'll get a move on."

He humphed. "You'd better, Tabitha Tweeter!" He shooed us along. "Now go!"

She gestured us to follow her, so we did, walking side by side down the darkened street.

"Tabitha Tweeter?" I asked.

She winced. "You can see why I don't introduce myself with my full name."

"Fair enough." I glanced at Cade. "You ever been here before?"

"Only a few times."

Despite the dark magic that hung on the air, his stride was relaxed. It made me twitchy, but apparently it wasn't enough to bother a god of war.

Tabitha led us past shops and pubs, most of which smelled or felt like dark magic. A few were more neutral, but they tended to deal in things that were iffier—like weapons and magical animals.

Right after we passed a man selling a potent brew out of a barrel around his neck, Tabitha stopped at a tall door.

Madame Mystical's Magical Mementos.

I looked at Tabitha. "We're going to see someone called Madame Mystical?"

"Yes. But if you call her that, you'll regret it."

Yeah, I wouldn't want to go by that name either.

"She inherited the shop from an ancestor. The same line of Eclektica has run this place for centuries. And it's been decades since a Madame Mystical has lived here. Just call her Melusine."

"Melusine, it is."

Tabitha pushed open the door and stepped inside. I followed with Cade close behind me.

A dozen scents and tastes bombarded me at once—magic of all varieties lived within this shop. The space towered at least three stories high, with shelves lining the walls all the way to the top. Thousands of magical objects sat on the shelves, each giving off their own signature.

The space in the middle was relatively empty: just a few display cases and some chairs. Near the domed ceiling, colorful birds fluttered. Or were they pixies? I squinted up, unable to see.

"Tabitha." The voice was deep for a woman's, and echoed with power.

I yanked my gaze from the pixies—definitely pixies—and sought out the voice.

The woman stood on the other side of the shop, leaning against a wide wooden desk with her arms crossed over her chest. She had flame red hair flowing in waves to her waist and wore a slinky red catsuit. Matching red heels gave her an extra four inches of height, which was impressive considering she was probably already five ten.

"Melusine." Tabitha grinned. "I brought you some customers."

Melusine waved her hand around the space. "Browse at your leisure. Haggle at your own risk."

"We're not here to browse." Though I did like the look of some of the books that were stacked against the shelf nearest to me. And there was a wicked-looking dagger that called my name. "We were sent here by Hedy. She said you could help us with a cursed portal."

Melusine's red eyebrows rose. "Now that sounds interesting."

She gestured me forward with nails that were tipped with black. They matched her eyes, which seemed to see straight through me.

We approached, dodging the cases of shrunken skulls and ancient genie lamps. As I neared, I got a hit of her magic signatures.

The scent of burning wood, the feel of a crackling fire warm on my face. I faltered just briefly.

Dang, she's strong. No wonder Hedy had sent us here.

CHAPTER FOUR

We stopped in front of Melusine, who never took her eyes from my face. It almost looked as if she recognized me.

Weird.

I didn't like it.

But I shrugged it off and dug into my pocket for the vial of oil that had been scooped off the front of the portal, and handed it over.

She reached for it, but instead of taking the vial, she grabbed my arm.

Her magic flared, suddenly feeling too hot against my face.

"Hey!" I yanked my arm back.

Cade stepped in front of me, jostling me out of the way. "Back up."

Melusine just laughed and stepped to the side, her dark eyes peering around Cade and landing on me. She smiled, a crafty, pleased smile that made me even more wary.

Then, she stepped back and sized up Cade. Her gaze widened with appreciation.

"Well, hello, god of war." She danced her fingers over his

chest. "I was so distracted by your friend Njord here that I didn't even notice you."

"Njord?" I asked.

But she ignored me, raking her gaze over Cade's tall form. What was it with all the ladies drooling over him? First the Vampire of Venice, and now Melusine?

Inwardly, I winced. I hadn't been much better. And it sure as heck wasn't my place to be jealous.

"Could you help us?" Cade asked. "We'll pay."

"Oh, and how?" she purred.

"Business, Melusine. We're here on business." Cade's voice was firm.

She rolled her eyes, then straightened. She snapped out her hand. "The vial, please."

Melusine was suddenly all business—as if a shutter had closed over her flirty side.

I handed it over, and she took it.

"Oh, interesting!" She raised it to her face and peered at it. "Right, let's go to the back. Tabitha? Will you flip the closed sign? Then you can go."

"On it." Tabitha waved goodbye to us, then hurried back to the door to do the job, and we followed Melusine toward the back of the room.

She led us through an arched blue doorway that led into a smaller round room. The ceiling was only two stories above us and domed like the one in the larger room. More pixies floated up there, darting around, their colorful wings blazing like rainbows.

"Illusions," Melusine said. "Cruel to keep pixies underground."

Well, at least she had a conscience.

There was a single round table in the middle of the space. It held a large stone basin that was round and shallow. Water gleamed on the surface. I felt a light tug in my chest, so subtle I thought I'd imagined it.

Weird.

I nodded toward the water. "This is all you use for your magic?" I'd never really heard of an Eclektica before.

"I am half Selkie. Hence, the basin of water. It helps me focus my power and read different magics. Create them."

Half Selkie? The sea creatures lived off the coasts of Ireland and Scotland, as far as I knew. And turned into seals. I wanted to ask her if she turned into a seal, but bit my tongue. Asking "do you put on a seal skin and flop into the sea at night?" was probably not polite.

Melusine approached the table and uncorked the vial. Cade and I joined her, standing on the other side of the table so we could get a good view.

She raised the vial to her nose and sniffed delicately, then grimaced.

"Rotten eggs, right?" I said.

"Yes. And evil." Her gaze met mine. "You said you need help with a portal?"

I nodded. "That stuff coats it. The portal has been closed for centuries, but now it's covered in that stuff and dark magic is seeping from it, poisoning the enchanted forest at the Undercover Protectorate."

"Oh, no good." She shook her head slowly as she poured some of the oil into the basin. It sank deep into the water, unfurling and spreading out like a cloud of darkness.

Melusine hovered her hand over the water, her magic flaring and her eyes glowing a bright silver.

She shuddered and stepped back, rubbing her palm against her sleek red catsuit. Her gaze landed on us. "Right. If you're going through that portal, you'll need something to protect you from this curse. I'm not sure exactly what it is, but it's destructive. Deadly for a human to be coated in that oil, I would imagine."

"Yeah, I don't want to sign up for that," I said.

"Can't say that I blame you." She walked toward a dark wooden door and pulled it open, riffling around for what I assumed were supplies. Then, she shut the door and turned to us. "I'll make you a spell that will temporarily protect you from the curse. But it'll cost."

Shit. Was this something that could be expensed to the Protectorate? Because I was pretty much broke at this point.

"That's fine," Cade said.

I'd have to ask Hedy or Jude about him getting paid back. Although he was an official member. He probably had that sorted.

"Step forward," Melusine said.

We did as she asked. She nodded at me. "You first."

I was about to ask what I needed to do when she raised a hand to my chest and hovered it near my heart. She dipped the fingertips of her other hand into the basin of water. Her palm near my chest glowed with red light, and something tugged within me. Then, she moved her hand toward the basin and dipped her fingers in. The glow sank into the inky black water and began to swirl around. It condensed into a tiny amount—no more than a cup—that was thick as oil and glowed red.

Melusine scooped it up in a little vial, then corked it and handed it to me. "Drink that before you go through the portal. It should last a few days."

I took it. The vial was warm against my hand.

She completed the same ritual with Cade, though his light glowed blue. Finally, she did a similar ritual with a key, dipping it into the remains of the oily water until it glowed gray.

She handed it to Cade. "This will help you unlock the portal. I'll send you a bill."

"Aye."

She escorted us from the room. The main shop was now empty, Tabitha gone.

"Thank you for the help." I nodded at her, then started for the door. Cade did the same.

"Hold your horses, Njord."

I turned to her. "Why do you keep calling me that?"

"That's something you need to figure out." She went to her desk and riffled through a drawer, then walked toward me. "Here."

She stuck out her hand. I reached to take whatever she was handing me, and she dropped a small golden stone onto my palm. "That'll let you come back here without an escort. If you need my help, come back."

"I need you to tell me why you're calling me Njord," I said. "That'd be pretty helpful."

"Frankly, I have no idea." She shook her head, confusion in her dark gaze. "But there's something strange about you. Almost recognizable."

Dang. That's not what I'd been hoping for.

"Thanks." I gave her one last, confused look, and turned. Cade waited for me by the door. I joined him.

"What did she give you?"

I held out my hand. The stone gleamed gold.

"That's quite an honor," he said.

"I'll take it." I shoved the stone in my pocket as we stepped out onto the darkened street. The Vaults were weird and creepy, but I kinda liked it. And a place like this could be useful.

We headed down the street, back toward the exit. The crowd had grown, as if they'd waited until night to come out. Music spilled from some of the bars, and shops bustled with customers.

It grew quieter toward the end of the street where Amos's shop and the bookstore were located. As we passed the alley that ran along the side of Amos's place, a rustling noise caught my ear.

I glanced down the alley just in time to see several figures dart away from the wall and kick down a side door. They rushed inside.

Adrenaline kicked into high gear, the memory of my own home being attacked by Ricketts and his gang spurring me on. Being attacked in your own home was the worst.

"Come on," I said. "Something's wrong."

"What?" Cade asked.

"Some people just broke into Amos's place." I darted down the alley, Cade behind me.

"Not friends of his?"

"Do you normally kick down the door when you visit your friends?"

"No." Cade drew his sword from the ether. "Would you like to lead or me?"

"Me." I liked that he immediately had my back.

We reached the small wooden door, which had been shut behind the intruders. But there was shouting coming from behind it.

I drew my sword from the ether and opened the door, rushing into the room.

It looked like a utility room, with a long counter and large sink on the back wall. Shelves with empty terrariums lined the other two walls. Two guys were smashing the terrariums while another had Amos in a headlock.

"You'll never get my shop!" the old man shouted.

Mobster bastards.

I didn't need to be from The Vaults to know what this was.

"Take the two smashing the place up," I said. "I've got Amos."

Cade darted toward the jerk who was so busy smashing stuff that he didn't even see us.

I shouted. "Hey! Pick on someone your own size!"

The guy strangling Amos looked up. He was skinny, with greasy blond hair and not much chin. His beady eyes landed on me and he snarled. "Who the hell are you?"

I immediately named him Rat Man, even though rats were way cuter than him.

"Your worst nightmare." I tried to give it my best Batman voice, but it really didn't work. "Just let go of Amos."

At my side, Cade had already knocked the first guy unconscious and was moving for the second. Rat Man's gaze darted to Cade and widened.

"Let go of Amos or he's on you next," I said. "Though it's actually me you should be concerned about."

Rat Man raised a dagger to Amos's throat. The old man paled.

"Let me outta here or the old man gets it." Rat Man's eyes were so wide and panicked that it looked like he'd just as easily mistakenly stab Amos.

If Cade turned on him, he'd probably freak. I could try throwing one of my daggers at him, but moving my arm that fast could startle him too. And my sonic boom was out of the question. It could pulverize Amos.

The sink behind him caught my eye, along with the tall faucet that gleamed in the dim light. Within, water waited.

I could feel it.

"Let me outta here!" Rat Man shrieked.

Yeah, he wasn't good under pressure.

Screw it.

I called on my new power over water—something I'd kept secret since I'd first used it in Venice—and imagined it shooting out of the faucet so hard it slammed Rat Man in the back of the head.

It did as I commanded. And I could *feel* it. Feel the pressure and the power. The faucet snapped and a jet of water sprayed out, hard enough to slam Rat Man in the back and throw him onto his front. He lost his grip on Amos, who stumbled to the side.

My gift over water was nothing like Caro's, who could slice through a man with the water she conjured out of the air.

Rat Man was still totally conscious and in one piece. He

groaned and scrambled to his feet, throwing out his hand and blasting his magic at me.

Green slime shot through the air and slammed against my chest. It burned like ant stings as it dripped down to my pants. "Ugh!"

Rat Man ran right for me, trying to get to the door.

I was so grossed out and annoyed that I dropped my sword and hit him with a right hook, smashing my fist into his jaw.

He stopped dead in his tracks, eyes rolling back in his head, and crashed into the ground.

Pain flared in my hand. I shook it. "Dang it!"

"My shop!" Amos yelled.

Cade dropped the unconscious vandal and strode toward the pipe that was still spurting water. He grabbed it and carefully squeezed it closed.

"Whoa," I muttered.

Cade turned to me. "Are you all right?"

"Yeah. Just stings like the devil." I tried to wipe the goop off me, flinging it to the ground. "Not acid, thankfully."

Amos approached, his wrinkled brow even more creased with confusion. He got right up close to me, peering up with bright eyes. "You are strange."

I stepped back. "Uh."

"There is magic within you that is not united." He sniffed, his nose wrinkling. "Aye. You must fix the conflict within you. Join the two halves, or you won't last long."

"What does that mean?"

He shrugged. "That's up to you to decide. But thank you for saving my shop." His gaze darted to the damaged water pipe, but he looked more resigned than angry. "If you ever decide you would like a pygmy toad, you come by. On the house."

"Thank you." I did *not* want a pygmy toad.

"What's going on here?" An authoritative voice sounded from behind me.

I turned, catching sight of a tall man with golden hair and blue eyes. He was handsome, if you were into Ken dolls.

I wasn't.

But he carried himself like a fighter, his broad shoulders and chest a clear indicator that he could throw down if necessary.

I didn't want to throw down. Not at the moment, at least. Not until after I'd had my shower.

"Lawman!" Amos hurried forward. "These good-for-nothing-no-good-miserable-sons-of-dogs came here and tried to scare me out of my shop!"

"Again?" The man shook his head. "You've got a valuable piece of real estate here, Amos." His gaze landed on us. He nodded at Cade, a respectful gesture, then looked at me. "And who are you?"

"Someone in need of a shower." I looked at Amos. "You all right?"

He nodded, clearly upset about his lost terrariums—for the pygmy toads, I had to assume—then he nodded toward the man he'd called Lawman. "He'll take it from here."

"Great." I gave a thumbs-up. "Then I'm outta here."

I needed a shower and I needed it quick. I left, passing by Lawman without making eye contact. I didn't want to meet anyone new, especially not someone going by the name Lawman. He might have something to do with the Order. Though I doubted it. He had more of a vigilante air about him.

Cade joined me out on the street, his gaze quickly taking in my soaked front. "Come on. I live close to here. You can get cleaned up."

I wanted to say that I'd do it back at the Protectorate, but honestly, this stuff burned like hell. "Thanks."

I followed him back through the exit and the book shop. As soon as we stepped onto the street, I sucked in a breath of cool, crisp air.

"This way." Cade led me down the street, going right and crossing the street toward a three-story building that looked to be at least a few hundred years old. We stopped in front of a green door. "This is my place."

He unlocked it, and we headed up three flights of stairs, entering another locked door.

"Bathroom is across the living room." He flipped on the lights to reveal a large space with a high ceiling and windows over-looking Edinburgh Castle. "I'll leave some clothes outside the door."

"Thanks." I raced across the living room, trying to take in as much as possible without dawdling. I was almost crawling out of my skin from the slime.

Cade's place was big and beautiful, filled with furniture that looked like a decorator had been told that Cade was masculine but classy, with a hint of the outdoorsman.

Which was accurate.

But it was the view that really got me. The castle, sitting high on the cliffs, glittered with golden light from the windows. I wanted to drift closer, take it all in.

No time for that, though.

I raced into the bathroom, which was spacious and modern, and cranked on the water, leaping beneath it without even taking off my boots.

I groaned. "Gonna regret that."

But at least the cool water was washing the slime away. I struggled out of my clothes, then scrubbed up with the soap that smelled like him. It wasn't the storm-at-sea scent of his magic, but something fresh and manly. Sandalwood?

Cade was clearly a dude's dude. But he carried it effortlessly, at least.

I scrubbed until all of the prickling sensation went away, then hopped out and dried off with one of his towels. A neatly folded pile of sweats sat on the floor outside the door, which I scooped up as fast as I could and then darted back into the bathroom.

As I pulled them on, I couldn't help but feel closer to him.

I was being weird.

This was the shit girlfriends did.

I was *so* not his girlfriend. Not even close.

I was the colleague who he had wisely rebuffed.

But that didn't stop me from raising the sweatshirt to my face and taking a big ol' whiff.

Then I stared into the mirror. "Idiot."

I shook my head, then tugged on my wet boots—*horrible*—and bent over to fish the golden stone out of the pocket of my discarded jeans. I tucked Melusine's gift into the big pocket on the sweatpants and hurried out of the bathroom. I'd have to ask for a plastic bag or something to deal with my gross clothes.

"Where are you?" I called.

The living room was located directly off the large entry foyer, but there were at least five doors leading out of the living room. Did he own the whole upper floor? What the heck did that cost in Scotland's capital city?

Nothing I could afford, that was for sure.

"In the kitchen," he called.

I followed his voice to the large archway on the left, near the windows. It led to a large kitchen that looked like it'd been recently remodeled. Wood and stone gleamed, and the breakfast table sported another great view of the castle.

"Who decorated this place? *Manly Man's Monthly?*" I asked.

"You just invented that."

"Indeed I did. It's a men's magazine for dudes who buy cologne that smells like aspen pine, fresh winter snow, and a hint of granite."

He laughed. "I don't know who decorated it. It came like this. But I like it." He studied me. "Feel better?"

"Yeah." I raised my arms. Eight inches of sweatshirt sleeve hung past my hands, which I shoved up to my elbows again. "Thanks for the clothes."

"It will do until we go back to the Protectorate." He reached for a plate on the counter, then handed it to me. "Eat this sandwich, then we'll go."

My stomach growled at the sight of the PB&J, and I took it. "Thanks. My favorite."

I chomped in, chewing happily.

"That was a good thing you did earlier today."

I swallowed, suddenly feeling awkward. "Wasn't going to leave an old man to get attacked."

"A lot of people would. Especially in a place like The Vaults."

"Well, I'm not a lot of people."

"No, you're not. You noticed the problem, acted quickly, and fixed the situation."

"You didn't mind following me in there."

"Why wouldn't I follow you in there?" He leaned against the counter, all powerful grace and easy confidence.

"Forget I asked." Because I understood now. Cade didn't mind following because he had nothing to prove.

There'd been a lot of men back in Death Valley who'd felt the need to prove the size of their balls. It *always* came in the form of patronizing bullshit and needing to be in charge and having the last word. They'd never have followed a *woman*.

Not Cade.

He wasn't a moron. And if you were a god of war, you probably lost any need to prove yourself to people or be the boss. You just *were* a badass. Which led to a level of chill that I liked.

Too much.

Of course.

The memory of our closeness back in the alley made heat rise in my cheeks. I shifted, preferring to study the view of the castle rather than Cade.

"You'll do well at the Protectorate," Cade said. "You're just the kind of person they're looking for. Strong, determined, competent."

My heart warmed. The guy knew how to compliment a woman. I'd been doubting myself, but maybe I shouldn't be. But it wasn't those words I latched onto. "Not *we*? You work there too."

"Not in the same way as the rest." He gestured to the apartment. "It's why I live here. I prefer to be on my own."

"I can see that." I wouldn't hate living here either. "Is it true you fight in battles around the world in your free time?"

"Sometimes." He shifted, clearly not wanting to talk about it, and reached into a drawer to retrieve a plastic grocery bag. He set it on the table. "You can pack up your clothes in that. Then we can get out of here."

I swallowed the last bit of the sandwich. "Thanks."

As I grabbed the plastic bag and retreated to the bathroom, I couldn't help but wonder why he was so reticent to talk about his good deeds. Didn't people normally do that? Why didn't he?

Ana was waiting for me when I returned to my apartment. She sat on the couch, next to Mayhem, the winged ghost pug who'd adopted me as her own. Unsurprisingly, Mayhem was chomping on a ham she'd found in the kitchen.

There seemed to be an endless supply of hams, just waiting for the pugs to snatch them.

Ana's brows rose at the sight of my oversized sweats, but I ignored her, diverting attention toward Mayhem instead. "Where the heck does she get all those hams? Shouldn't the kitchen have figured it out by now that the Pugs of Destruction are going to steal them?"

"I'm more interested in how a ghost dog can eat a real ham," Ana said. "But don't change the subject. Why are you wearing Cade's clothes?"

"Don't get excited." I tossed my bag of slimy clothes onto the side table and set down the golden stone Melusine had given me. "I got slimed."

Ana winced. "Did you figure out how to get through the portal?"

"Someone briefed you?" I hadn't had time to talk to her before I'd left for Edinburgh.

"Word gets around."

"Yeah. We're going in tomorrow morning at dawn."

"I hate that you're going alone."

"It's just recon. When we need backup, you'll be the first in." I took the middle seat on the couch, between her and Mayhem. Fortunately, the pug had mastered a strange way of eating that kept the ham from touching the couch. She might be a Pug of Destruction, but she wasn't going to waste any precious ham juice on my upholstery. Since it was the first nice thing I owned, I appreciated it.

I rubbed her back, not really making contact since she was a ghost. But it was nice, in a tingly way.

"I was hoping you could do me a favor while I'm on recon," I said.

"Anything." Ana turned toward me, giving me a full view of the sleeping ducks on her giant night shirt.

"I'm starting to get some clues about what I am, but I have no idea what they mean. Can you find the library and do some research like we talked about?"

"Of course. What have I got to go on?"

"I've been called Njord—whatever that means. And this strange old man in Edinburgh said that I have conflict within me that must be resolved. Two halves that must be made whole."

"All right. Not a bad start."

I leaned back against the couch and stared up at the wooden ceiling. "I sure hope you can find something. Because this is starting to get scary."

Ana reached for my hand and squeezed. "We can handle it."

CHAPTER FIVE

Cade and I met early the next morning in the entryway of the castle. Though we had full kitchens in our apartments, I'd figured out early that there was a large communal kitchen on the first floor of the castle. A man named Hans was the head cook, and he made a mean cup of coffee.

Before meeting Cade, I'd swung by there to grab a cup, and I was pretty sure it was the only thing keeping me standing. It was quiet this close to dawn, and no one in their right minds was awake.

"Ready?" Cade asked as I stepped into the entry hall.

He wore a backpack and was dressed in boots, and his dark clothes looked like they were made of sturdy fabric. Exploration gear, if I'd ever seen it.

"Yep, ready."

Footsteps sounded from behind me, and I turned to see Jude descending the sweeping staircase on the left. She had a paper clutched in her hand. "I have a copy of that map here for you. If you're not back in three days, we'll send reinforcements in after you."

"Thanks." I took the map that she handed me. "We'll figure this out."

She nodded. "See that you do. Passing this test will go a long way toward advancing you at the Academy. And from a practical standpoint, that portal is a *serious* problem."

I nodded, feeling the pressure of the real-life test, and turned to Cade. "Ready to get a move on?"

"Aye."

We said goodbye to Jude, then strode from the castle and across the lawn. The sun was peaking over the horizon by the time we reached the forest, though it was still dark within. The fairy lights helped illuminate the path, and made the nippy air feel just a bit warmer.

When we reached the clearing, I raised my hand over my nose. "The smell is worse."

"Aye." Cade's voice hinted at his disgust.

"And the curse has spread farther." The black veins stretched across the forest floor, all the way to the edge of the clearing. "We need to hurry."

I pulled the vial of potion that Melusine had given me and downed it quickly, wincing at the taste of sour milk. "Ugh."

A cold chill raced over my skin, followed by a tingling sensation. Hopefully, that meant the potion was working.

Cade drank his, then pulled the big key Melusine had given him from his pocket. He held it up and gave me an inquiring look. "Ready?"

"Let's do it."

My heart thudded as we approached the portal. The surface gleamed like an oil slick, and the memory of the creature pressing out of it made my skin chill with nerves.

I called one of my daggers from the ether, gripping it like a security blanket.

Cade raised the key to the portal and pressed it into the oily surface. There was no distinct keyhole, but the portal shimmered. He twisted the key.

The portal glowed white, just briefly.

"Go." Cade pulled the key from the portal and stepped through, disappearing.

"Now or never." I sucked in a deep breath and followed.

My skin crawled as I passed through, feeling like tarantulas were scuttling over my flesh. A shudder raked me as I stepped out onto a dimly lit beach, joining Cade.

The sun was just starting to peek out from behind some clouds on the horizon, sending a hazy gray morning light over the waves and hard-packed sand. A forest to the left looked dark and abandoned. Sick, almost. The ocean to the right was gray and dark, waves lapping at the shore.

A rustling sounded from behind me, and I whirled.

A slimy pitch-black creature—shaped kind of like my imaginings of an alien—lunged for me. Its skin gleamed with the same oil that covered the portal, and there were no eyes in its elongated head.

Right before it reached me, I hurled my dagger. It thudded into the creature's skinny chest. The beast, which was well over six feet tall, wobbled, then reached out with a slender, claw-tipped arm. I lunged backward, but the monster was fast. It sliced through my arm.

Pain flared.

I stumbled backward, drawing my sword from the ether.

But Cade was faster. He lunged forward, sword and shield in hand. The creature sliced out again, but Cade blocked with his shield. The beast's hand clanged against the metal, as if it, too, were made of iron. Cade sliced his blade clean through its neck.

The head crashed to the ground, exploding in a puddle of oil, and the body followed shortly after.

"Thanks." I gasped, catching my breath, and pressed my hand

against the wound on my arm. It was so thin that it barely bled, thank fates, but it stung like the devil. Warily, I approached the fallen body. It had splashed into a pile of oil, though it'd felt solid when it was attacking. "What is it? It didn't really seem alive, did it?"

I hadn't noticed it breathe. Or seen its chest move. And it'd made no sound.

Cade nudged the oil puddle with his blade. "A spell. Or some other kind of monster. It's not disappearing the way demons do."

I turned from it and spun in a circle, inspecting the beach. It stank like rotten eggs, and there was a gray tinge over the land. Black veins spread across the ground, just like the ones that were starting to infect the castle.

"The poison is still here," I said. "Killing the creature didn't change that."

Cade chuckled. "That would be too easy." He knelt down and touched one of the black veins that shot through the hard-packed sand. "The beast was a symptom, not the cause."

"Think there are more?" I squinted into the forest, which looked haunted as hell. Twisted trees reached for the sky, their leafless branches barren and dead.

"Could be."

I unfolded the map Jude had given us. It was sparsely drawn with very little detail. "There's almost nothing on this map."

"The Fae who once lived here did not permit the Protectorate much access, from what I've heard. They were a suspicious people."

"Clearly." The mapmaker looked like he'd drawn the thing from quick memory after a brief visit. It looked like there was a settlement of some kind, past the beach and forest and an open space. I pointed to it. "What do you say we look for answers there?"

"I'd say that's a good idea."

We'd have to be sneaky since we didn't know what kind of welcome we'd get, but going toward people was the best chance at getting answers. And I was doubtful that the Fae were behind this. Why would they want to contact me?

The sand stretched out far ahead of us, the haunted forest on the left and the dark gray ocean on the right.

"Too bad we can't transport."

"If we knew exactly where it was, we could." Cade patted the left pocket of his trousers. "But I do have a transportation charm in case we get into serious trouble. We'll come straight back to the portal and return to the Protectorate."

"Sounds good." I looked around. "I wonder if this dark magic is what made the Fae close their portal? Or if it's new."

"The speed with which it is infecting the enchanted forest at the Protectorate leads me to think it *is* new."

"Good point." I set off down the beach. It was exposed, which I didn't love, but I was staying away from that forest and we had no boat to travel on the water. Not like I'd want to, anyway.

Cade joined me, matching his stride to mine. Eventually, I became used to the stink of rotten eggs.

We walked in companionable silence for a while. It worked for me, since silence made it easier not to put my foot in my mouth. I couldn't help but still be attracted to him. Except he'd made it very clear how well that was going to work out.

The sun climbed higher in the sky as we crossed the long beach. Eventually, a forest appeared at the far end.

I rubbed my chest, suddenly feeling something strange.

Like an awareness. A heaviness.

My gaze darted to the sea. It called to me, almost as if I could hear the siren song.

Holy fates. Was I feeling the sea?

Nah.

I tried to shake it away.

"Do you hear that?" Cade murmured.

"What?" I was so preoccupied with the ocean that I hadn't been paying attention.

"In the forest. A rustling noise."

"Great." I inspected it as I walked, tracing my gaze over the large, dead trees. There were still a few green ones left here and there, but most were withered and leafless. Black veins crept up their trunks, strangling the life from them. "I don't see anything."

A rumbling from my right pulled my gaze over to the sea. The waterline was pulling back from the shore! The beach was now twice as wide.

"Cade!"

He turned toward the sea, eyes widening. "Shite! Run."

I whirled and sprinted toward the forest, away from the receding ocean. I'd only ever heard of the sea receding in two cases—right before hurricanes and tidal waves. Either way, I wanted to be a hell of a lot farther from the water.

Whatever was rustling in the forest was about to get some company.

My breath heaved in my lungs as I ran. We were still fifty yards from the trees. When the roaring of the sea increased, I chanced a glance backward.

My heart leapt into my throat and my skin chilled to ice.

A massive tidal wave loomed overhead, bearing down on us. It rose over a hundred feet in the air, gray and dark.

Shit!

We'd never make it to the trees. Not that they could really help.

"Cade!" On instinct, I lunged for him, wrapping my arms around his waist and taking us both to the sand.

The wave crashed down on us, a force so powerful that I lost my hearing and my vision as it sucked us up and tossed us around like dolls. My blood thundered in my veins, and my head roared as I thrashed around in the water. Cold. It was so cold.

Fear like I'd never known caught me in a vise. Cade's strong arms wrapped around my waist. He was kicking, trying to reach the surface that we couldn't see.

The water surrounded me. Crushing. Seeping inside me.

I could *feel* it.

No way was I going to drown. Not in the ocean.

The idea was freaking ridiculous, for some reason.

I forced the water away from me, envisioning it retreating.

Go, go, go.

Away!

I had no idea if it was working. Everything was gray and dark, and my lungs burned as we were thrashed about in the sea.

Then I hit solid ground. The water rushed off me. I lay limp against the wet sand, choking on water. I rolled away from Cade, weakly retching up the water. Beneath my hands, the sand was wet and covered in a fine layer of sea grass.

I sucked in a ragged breath, coughing.

The air rushing into my lungs was the best feeling in the world.

Beside me, Cade coughed and gasped.

I looked up, having no clue what had just happened.

We were surrounded on all sides by walls of water that rose fifty feet high. The blue sky filled the hole above our heads, and the sun shined down into the water, making it glint blue from this angle.

"Holy fates." I scrambled upright, whirling around in a circle to take it all in.

There were fish in the water, staring at us like they were in an aquarium. Or like we were in an aquarium. Giant coral heads dotted the ground around us, white and red and yellow. There were even a couple of sharks staring right at me through the wall of water.

At my feet, a squishy white thing flopped around.

Holy fates!

An octopus.

I grabbed the thing up, wincing at the slimy feel of its skin, and ran for the wall of water. I thrust the octopus into it. Immediately, the creature poofed up, regaining its proper form now that it was submerged. I released it and yanked my hand back out. The octopus darted away.

"What the hell is happening?" Cade asked.

I stepped away from the wall of water—and the Hammerhead who was looking at me like I was a tasty snack—and joined Cade in the middle of our air-filled cylinder.

"I have no idea." I couldn't take my gaze off the sea around us. Or the sky above.

"Do you have any idea how to get us out of it?"

"Our options aren't great." We couldn't climb the walls of water. Nor did I want to walk into the water and try to swim my way up. It'd be fifty feet to the surface, and the sharks could get us. Not to mention, if this water collapsed, we were screwed.

"You're holding it back," he said. "Can you clear another path toward the shore?"

"Maybe?" I could feel the water—like it was part of me. It took hardly any effort at all to hold it like this. "But which way is shore?"

"Bree. Turn around." His voice had the calm steadiness of someone who knew something was going wrong.

I turned to face the direction he was pointing. The water shimmered on that side. Figures walked toward us along the bottom of the sea. Nine of them. Women.

They stepped out of the wall of water, entering our air bubble. Each was made of shimmering blue water, but their features and hair and clothes were so detailed that they looked real.

My head spun.

"They are not the Fae," Cade said.

I'd seen some crazy shit in the magical world, but this was *beyond*.

Awkwardly, I raised a hand and waved. "Hi."

Fortunately, Cade didn't draw his sword from the ether. Not like it'd do much good against an army of water women.

They approached gracefully, the sun gleaming off their shimmery water surfaces, and stopped in front of us, forming a semicircle.

All their eyes were on me.

"Who are you?" one asked.

"Um, Bree Blackwood." I hiked a thumb toward Cade. "And this is Cade, the Celtic god of war."

They didn't look at him, just crowded closer. I could see confusion on their faces, which was a bit weird considering I could also see *through* their faces.

"Who are you?" I asked. "Why are we here?"

"We brought you here," said the leader.

"We wanted to know more." The one to her left leaned closer, squinting at my face. Then she turned to the leader. "I think you're right, Hefring. I can sense Rán in her."

"Rán?" I asked.

"Our mother." The leader nodded. "It is finally time."

The others began to chatter in an unknown language, voices rising over top of each other.

"Time for what?" I asked.

"Only you can determine that. But you must leave here to do so." Hefring raised her arms.

Sloshing water sounded from behind me. My heart leapt into my throat and I turned. The water parted, forming an air channel back to shore.

I spun back to Hefring. "Who is Rán? What's happening to me?"

"You must go," Helga said. "The passage won't stay open long."

"But—"

"Come, sisters." Hefring stepped back toward the ocean. Her eight siblings followed, joining her in the water. They walked off, accompanied by a procession of sharks.

"Come on." Cade grabbed my hand and tugged me along.

I gave one last longing look after Hefring and her sisters, then turned and ran. We sprinted down the channel, between the tall walls of water that housed fish who watched our progress.

My lungs burned as we ran, but I pushed myself harder, not wanting to get caught if the sea slammed back down upon us. I could control it—yes. But I didn't fully trust myself.

As if on cue, the water began to crash down behind us, driving us on.

Hefring encouraging me to get a move on? I could almost feel her presence as I sprinted, lungs burning.

We sprinted onto the dry beach—the *real* beach—as the sea splashed down, returning to normal. I stumbled, going to my knees in the sand, and barely caught myself with my hands.

I hung my head, panting, wet hair hanging in my face.

Holy fates. This was nuts.

I flopped onto my back, staring up at the blue sky. Cade lay next to me, arm thrown above his head as his big chest heaved up and down.

"That was wild," I finally said.

"That was insane." He rolled over to look at me, propping himself on an elbow so he leaned overtop of me. "Are you all right?"

Concern glinted in his gaze. His wet sweater clung to the muscles of his chest and arms, while his dark hair glittered with water droplets that gleamed in the sun. Worse, his full lips were damp.

My gaze went straight to them.

Oh, fates.

That near-death experience should have killed any desire I had lurking inside me.

As if.

I was a danger junkie. Fear fueled me. And so did Cade.

The combo? Explosive.

I licked my lips and drew in an unsteady breath. Cade's hot gaze dropped to my mouth. The heat in his eyes made me burn.

Yes.

I wanted to lean up. Press my lips to his. But no matter how much I wanted him—and damn it, I knew he wanted me too—there was no way I was going to kiss him.

Memory of my last attempt kept me pinned to the ground.

"Um, I—" My mind scrambled for any words.

Shutters fell over Cade's eyes. He leaned back and sat up, resting his arms over his knees. I heaved myself up beside him, staring out at the now calm sea.

"I don't know why I can control the water," I said. "But the power is new."

He nodded. "We'll sort it out."

I hoped so.

Cade pulled the pack off his back, opened it, and riffled through the contents. "Well, the food is mostly shot. I hope you like salty apples and granola bars, because that's all that wasn't ruined."

"How long will that last us?"

"It'll get unpleasant after a day. But we may find food. Or help."

"Here's hoping." I struggled to my feet, muscles aching and chest still on fire. Gingerly, I reached into my pocket and found the wet map. I unfolded it, grateful for the sturdy paper. Still in pretty good condition. "Let's get a move on. There's still a long way to go."

We started down the beach again, our clothes drying in the warm sun.

"You have more control over the water than you do your sonic boom power," Cade said.

"I know." It'd been worrying me. "And it's weird. The changes have been happening fast. I had good control when you created that creepy monster, but other times it's shot." I looked at him. "I know you trust me in a pinch. But I honestly don't know if my magic can stand up to the challenge anymore."

"You're more than just your magic, Bree. That challenge was meant to prove you can do it. But if your gift changes, you'll adapt."

A small smile tugged at my lips. Why did he have to be so great?

I turned and quickened my pace. Finally, we reached the end of the beach. It butted up to a dark forest. I sniffed, nose wrinkling. "Still stinks."

"Rotten eggs and something else..." Cade's brow wrinkled as he thought. "Blood?"

"Ugh." I searched the forest. The trees were closely spaced, and their bark was black. Whether it was natural or a disease, I couldn't tell.

I dug out the map and carefully unfolded it. "We're nearly halfway there. We go through the forest, then the Fae city is in the clearing beyond that."

Cade nodded and stepped into the forest.

I followed.

Immediately, it was quieter. There was no gentle roar of the ocean waves, and the temperature dropped considerably without the sun.

I looked up. Frowned. "There are no leaves on these trees."

"Yet it's still dark."

"I don't like it."

"Neither do I. Stay close." He drew his sword from the ether.

I followed suit. I could try my sonic boom here, but my blade was always handy. And there was no water other than the ocean. Soon, it'd be too far away to call upon.

We walked as silently as we could, cutting between the trees and avoiding the bark that looked sharp-edged. There was no path from what I could tell.

Did the Fae ever use this forest?

Not from what I could see.

A rustling sounded at my left. My heart jumped, and I glanced over, searching between the trees.

"I see nothing," Cade murmured.

"Neither do I." But it *definitely* sounded like something was there.

Cade picked up the pace and I followed. We'd gone about two miles in when the smell began to change. It was more coppery. More—

"Blood." I gazed in horror at the tree nearest me.

Crimson liquid was dripping down the blackened bark, pooling on the ground below. It smelled like blood.

"Don't touch it." Cade jumped over a puddle of shining red liquid that had seeped onto the forest floor. I followed, sticking close by his side.

I kept my grip loose on my sword, ready to swing.

The forest grew darker as we got deeper in, the trees closer and the rustling sounds more distinct. There were rock outcroppings here and there, large granite boulders that cast shadows on the ground.

My hair stood on end and my senses were as alert as a cat burglar's.

"Duck!" a strange voice shouted.

It was so intense, so serious, that I followed instinctually. Cade did too.

We ducked low as a man made of rocks hurtled toward us, then leapt over our heads.

CHAPTER SIX

My heart thundered as I whirled around to see what the hell had just happened.

A man—at least, I *thought* he was a man, since he was made entirely of rough stone—fought a giant hairy winged thing.

I stumbled back, side to side with Cade.

"What the hell?" I asked.

"I think the rock man is on our side." Cade winced as the rock swung his heavy fist at the creature's head and removed half its skull.

The hairy winged thing flew to the side and slammed against a tree. Dead.

The rock stepped back, dusting his hands together in a move that said *job well done.*

I peered at the creature, realizing it was a giant bat-like thing. Huge fangs protruded from its mouth. Blood began to seep from every inch of its skin, flowing into the ground, which drank it up like a sponge. The bat shrank down to nothing.

"Ew!" I grimaced.

"Yeah, not pretty, those VDBs." The rock man sounded like a

teenager with a slightly strange accent. New Zealand-ish almost. "Murderous pests, is what they are."

"VDBs?" I asked.

Rock man turned to us and smiled. He was about the size of Cade. But yeah, he looked like a kid. Or at least, as much as a rock figure could look like a kid.

"Vampire Demon Bats, the scourge of this fair land." He swept out his arm to indicate the creepy forest. "You've never seen one before?"

"No," Cade said. "We're not from around here."

"Well, I coulda told you that. Ain't nothing but rocks from here to the abandoned city. The VDBs saw to that."

I stepped forward and held out my hand. This kid was going to be our ally, if I had anything to say about it. "I'm Bree Blackwood. Thanks for taking out the VDB."

He nodded and smiled, then stuck his hand toward mine. He gripped it gently, as if consciously trying not to pulverize my bones. "I'm Rocky. Good to meet ya."

Rocky. How fitting.

"I'm Cade." He stepped forward and shook Rocky's hand.

"So, what are you two doing here? Haven't seen a Breather in a couple hundred years, at least."

"Breathers are humans?" I asked.

"And Fae. Anyone not made of rock that walks on two legs. And breathes."

"Where are the Fae?" Cade asked. "Isn't this their land?"

"*Was* their land." Rocky hiked a thumb toward the withered corpse of the VDB. "Until those bastards showed up. Drove the Fae off about three hundred years ago. Nothing but outcasts living in their city now."

I glanced at Cade. Three hundred years was about the time that the Fae portal had closed. And if there were only outcasts left, we didn't have to worry about inciting a war, at least.

"Is that why they closed their portal to the Undercover

Protectorate?" I asked.

"Wouldn't know nothing about that." Rocky shrugged. "I'm only two hundred years old. Just a kid, according to me mum. But yeah, safe to assume they didn't want the VDB to get through to you. Did you a favor right before they ran for it."

Cade rubbed a hand over his jaw. "So they just disappeared."

"Ran off. Those that weren't killed, at least. Can't kill me though. I'm a rock. Ain't got nothing the VDBs want."

I looked around at the miserable forest. "Isn't it lonely out here?"

"Nah. I got my family. They're rocks, too, so they made it out okay. Can't kill rocks."

Right. Of course. He had a way of stating the obvious that was somehow charming. "Do the VDBs have anything to do with the dark curse that's spreading from this world and out through the portal into ours? And the oily black monster that was near the portal?"

Rocky shook his head. "Don't think so. This blackness came after the VDB. A while."

"How much later?" Cade asked.

"Don't know. Not so good with time. I'm a rock. Rocks can't tell time."

I chuckled softly. Rocky liked to be precise, that I could tell. But at least we knew the two were separate—and this new problem hadn't destroyed the Fae.

"We're looking for the source of the new dark magic," I said. "Do you know where it's coming from?"

"Not a clue. Just showed up one day. But the people in the old Fae city might know."

"Can you take us there?" Cade asked. "Show us the lay of the land, so we don't run into any more VDBs?"

Rocky grinned wide, clearly delighted to be asked. "Not a problem. Long as I'm home for dinner."

"Wait—what do rocks eat?" I asked.

"Nothing." Rocky shrugged. "But me mum learned it from the Fae before they left. She likes the tradition. So we all sit around the log and look at each other."

"All right, then. Back by dinner, it is." I clapped my hands once. "Let's go."

"This way." Rocky started off through the trees in the direction we'd been headed.

While we would probably eventually find the city on our own, it was much better to have a guide.

"Good job getting us an escort," I whispered to Cade.

"I like the kid."

"Me too."

As we walked, Rocky rambled on about the dangers in the forest—which he seemed to regard as something like his own personal video game.

"So, you like it here?" I asked.

"Oh yeah, love it. The VDBs may have made life a nightmare for the Fae, but they're downright entertaining for us."

"Everyone needs a hobby." I jumped over a puddle of blood, trying not to look too closely at it.

"Did the new poisonous oil make the trees bleed?" I asked.

"No, that's the VDBs. They become one with the forest when they die, giving it their blood. Not much I can tell you about that oil stuff. Hasn't been around long."

"For a rock, *long* could mean anything from weeks to a few years, right?"

Rocky nodded, smiling. "Now you're getting it."

I pointed to a bubbling yellow river ahead. It was about a hundred feet across and stank like sewage. "What's that?"

"The bubbly pit. Don't want to get that stuff on you," Rocky said. "Melt right through your clothes."

"Through rock, too?"

"Yep. Through granite. My Uncle Al lost a finger that way. Uncle Al never was the smartest." He stopped at the edge of the pool and pointed to the rocks dotting the way across. "But you can jump on those fellas. They're my buddies. They don't mind."

"Why aren't they dissolved?" I asked.

"Different kind of rock. This is like a steam bath to them." Rocky waved. "Hey, fellas! We're just gonna cross, all right?"

One of the rocks rose up slightly. It was a head. "Sure thing, Rocky." The rock creature's gaze landed on me. "You hanging out with Breathers?"

"Visitors. Ain't it the thing?"

The rock grunted, then slipped back below the water.

"He's not going to throw me off, is he?" I asked.

"Ha!" Rocky slapped his knee, as if that had been a hilarious joke. "Nah, Boulder liked you. That was friendly, for him."

I glanced at Cade, who shrugged and nodded. "I'll go first."

"Nope. Me, my good man. Follow my lead." Rocky stepped onto the first rock, then began to hop his way across.

We followed, Cade going before me.

The stench was eye-watering as we leapt from stone to stone. My muscles ached from the strain of maintaining my balance. By the time we reached the other side, sweat was dripping down my temples.

"Not bad, eh?" Rocky grinned. "My best time is forty-five seconds, but you weren't too slow."

"Thanks." I saluted.

"This way." Rocky turned and set off through the forest.

We followed. This side didn't look any better than the other—same bleeding trees and dark sky. By the time the growls and hisses started up in the distance, I was almost relieved. I'd been on edge, waiting for another monster.

"Oh, this is a treat!" Rocky said.

Sure, Rocky. I didn't know what was making that noise, but I sure as heck wanted my sword. Cade seemed to agree, because he drew his at the same time.

Rocky turned to us, his expression clearly aghast. "No

swords!"

I frowned at him. "Sounds like a pretty ferocious beast."

"Nah, not if you know how to treat 'em right."

At that moment, five huge, rat-like creatures crept out of the bush. They had scraggly black fur and blazing red eyes, along with whiskers that were at least two feet long. Their lips were pulled back from yellow fangs as they hissed and spat. The largest one was growling like a washing machine full of screws.

"Hey, fellas!" Rocky waved at the rats, which didn't so much as look at him. "I know, I know. Treatie time!"

I shifted closer to Cade, so we could fight back-to-back if necessary.

Rocky just ignored us, going over to one of the large trees and leaping up to pull off one of the withered fruits. He tossed the dark gray thing at the nearest rat, which leapt into the air and snagged it with yellow fangs. It tore into the fruit like it had to break its neck.

Rocky repeated the drill, tossing withered fruits to the rats, which couldn't get enough. Their eyes calmed down to a dull, red color—no longer flaming—and the hisses and growls eventually stopped.

I lowered my sword.

Rocky turned to us, a smile on his face. "Mice love apples."

A laugh escaped me. "Those are neither mice nor apples, but whatever. Good job, Mouse Whisperer."

Rocky's grin spread wider on his face and he turned. "We're almost there. Let's get out of here before the mice finish their treaties. They get moody after that."

I glanced at the enormous devil rats who were massacring their withered fruits, then hurried after Rocky and Cade.

"Did the mice come with the VDBs?" I asked.

"Nah, according to me mum, they used to pull the Fae chariots. Now they're kinda wild, rampaging through the forest, looking for treaties."

Considering I was frequently on the hunt for a nice pink cocktail, I couldn't blame them.

After walking for another forty minutes, the trees began to thin.

"Almost there," Rocky said. We reached the edge of the tree line, which looked out onto a wide-open plain. Rocky pointed. "Just beyond the horizon is the village. Be careful, though. They don't love visitors. I'd take you, but it's almost dinnertime."

"We will." I turned to him. "Thanks, Rocky."

Cade thanked him too.

"Glad to do it." He grinned. "Stop by and see me again. I'll show you Razor Mountain."

I gave him a thumbs-up. "For sure."

Lie. Big, fat lie. As much as I'd like to see Rocky again, I didn't want to get anywhere near Razor Mountain.

He saluted, then ran off into the woods. Before he disappeared through the trees, he turned around and shouted, "Oh yeah, and watch out for the VDBs!"

Great.

I turned to Cade. "Ready for this?"

He rubbed his hands together and smiled. "Looking forward to it."

I nodded and conjured my sword and shield. Cade did the same, though his weapons were far larger than mine.

I sucked in a bracing breath. "Let's go."

We started across the sandy expanse. The ground was hard-packed and dusty out here, away from the forest. It was a totally different ecosystem from the last two we'd just been in. Bright sun shined down. Nothing like Death Valley, but I'd have preferred the cover of night.

When the first shriek sounded in the distance, my heartrate spiked.

I glanced around, catching sight of the oncoming VDB. It was huge—the size of a horse—with massive fangs and blazing red eyes. The stench of its magic reached me from far away.

"Got this one." Cade didn't break his stride as he drew his arm back and hurled his shield.

The shining silver metal flew through the air so fast it was hard to see, and collided with the bat. The beast tumbled through the air, and the shield returned to Cade.

Nice.

I kept up the pace, my breath coming short. I was more used to riding than running.

The next bat came out of nowhere. I barely heard the flap of wings in time. I ducked, and the beast sailed over me. Cade threw his shield, taking it out.

The third was mine. It flew from the left, hurling toward me with a bloodthirsty glint in its eyes. When it was close enough for me to see the hairs on its hide, I stabbed with my sword. The blade sank into the creature's belly, and it tumbled to the ground.

I kept sprinting, occasionally cutting down VDBs as Cade knocked more out of the sky with his shield.

My lungs burned and my legs ached, but soon, there was a massive city on the horizon. It rose tall and pale, a strange conglomeration of buildings built out of the earth. They all looked to be stacked on top of each other, making a city that was more vertical than horizontal.

We were still a few miles away, but this wasn't going so bad.

"Incoming!" Cade shouted. "From behind."

I turned to look.

Shit.

I'd spoken too soon. A horde of VDBs darkened the sky, hurtling toward us from the forest. As if someone had told them that a snack waited for them out on the planes, without even a tree for shelter.

The stench of their magic filled the air as they flew toward us, their red eyes blazing.

The ground rumbled, sending vibrations through my legs.

Then the ground in front of me dropped away, leaving a two-foot-wide crevasse. I leapt over it, fear chilling my skin.

But the ground kept rumbling, dropping away in sections as the bats gained on us.

Oh, we are so screwed.

I sprinted harder, but there was no way I could outrun the bats. And the crevasses in the sand were getting wider and wider.

"Hang on!" Cade stashed his sword and shield in the ether, and his magic flared around him.

He never stopped running, but a moment later, a massive wolf was loping along in his place. The beast was four times the size of a normal wolf, with rippling muscles and a sleek, silvery-gray coat.

It swerved toward me, green eyes intent on my face, and jerked its head.

Get on.

Holy fates.

The message was clear. Cade wanted me to ride on his back.

No way.

The ground dropped away in front of me, creating the widest gap I'd seen yet. Cade leapt over it with ease, but I barely made it.

Behind me, the bats shrieked.

I glanced behind.

They were so close now. And the ground rumbled.

"All right!" I called.

Cade slowed beside me, and I stashed my sword and shield in the ether. I jumped onto his back, grabbing the scruff of his fur and hauling my leg over his side.

He was so warm, his heat sinking through to my skin. I could feel the ripple of muscle as he ran, his great paws eating up the ground as he bounded over giant crevasses. I crouched low, hanging on for dear life, and he hurtled over the ground. My leg muscles burned as I clutched his sides.

Every time he leapt over a newly formed crevasse, I felt like I might tumble off him.

The scent of his magic wrapped around me, a storm at sea that was so at odds with this strange desert environment. The taste of fresh apples exploded on my tongue, and the sound of swords clashing in battle rang in my ears. It felt like I was within his magic shield.

A sense of goodness and honor flowed through me. It was *him.*

I could feel who he was—everything that made him special. This was the main reason people *never* rode Shifters. It was too intimate. Too personal.

The VDBs shrieked again, a cacophony that was like a battle cry.

I clung to Cade and turned my head, catching sight of the horde of them. They were hunting as a pack, and their hungry red eyes were on us.

Fight.

I could hear Cade in my mind. Not quite telepathy. More a joining of the souls—two people who knew how to fight and what must be done. Maybe the Shifter thing gave us a greater connection. I had no idea.

I drew in a ragged breath and let go of the scruff of his neck, slowly raising myself from a crouch.

The ground whizzed by beneath us, making my stomach drop.

I was going to have to turn around to fight the VDB.

Oh fates, this sucked. But the bats were coming from behind. As quickly as I could, I scrambled around, finally facing back toward the forest.

And the VDBs.

They were only twenty yards off now.

I clutched Cade's sides with my legs as I drew my sword and shield from the ether.

Focus on those.

The cold steel was comforting beneath my hands. Much better than the sight of the ground and frequent crevasses. I could fall off any moment and plummet into the earth.

Yep. Better to focus on stabbing the VDBs.

The first VDB dived, shooting toward me like a missile. I swung, slicing across its neck and sending it tumbling through the air.

The next came from the left. I stabbed it in the throat with my sword, gagging at the scent of its rotten blood. A third bat came from the right.

Too soon.

I raised my shield as I yanked my blade from the throat of the other VDB. The monster plowed into the shield, sending me careening to the side.

I clutched hard with my legs, barely managing to stay on.

"Faster!" I cried.

Cade put on a burst of speed, racing across the plains like a beast possessed. I clung to his back as I fought off the VDBs, slicing and stabbing as the monsters attacked from all angles.

Sweat dripped down my face and stung my eyes, but the attack slowed as I took out more and more. Finally, the last VDB thudded to the earth.

I sagged on top of Cade, stashing my sword and shield in the ether and holding on to his back for support. My legs felt like jello, weak from clinging to him.

Behind us was a trail of broken ground and VDB corpses. Their blood soaked into the earth as they disappeared, leaving no trace that they'd ever existed.

Panting, I kept my arms wrapped around Cade's waist. His fur smelled divine. Like his stormy magic and whatever soap he used.

Honestly, I probably liked this too much.

Finally, he slowed. I straightened on his back, looking behind me to see how close we were to the Fae settlement.

Nearly there.

It was the strangest place I'd ever seen. A city made entirely of packed sand, from what I could tell. It rose at least six stories into the sky, but the whole place was like some fantastic, jumbled high-rise. It was actually many buildings all piled on top of each other with stairs and passages winding throughout. Very maze-like. Very Fae. I'd forgotten to ask what kind of Fae they were, but maybe a desert variety.

Cade slowed to a halt at the edge of the city.

I leapt off his back, stumbling as I hit the ground.

He leaned toward me, and I grabbed the fur at his side, steadying myself.

Fae magic drifted from the place, smelling of the forest and sea and desert. It brushed across my skin like a feather and pricked like nettles. It sounded like a crackling fire and the roar of wind.

"Lots of magic here," I murmured. The place looked abandoned, but the magic belied that. There were thousands of places to hide, anyway. I could only see the outer edge of the city. There was much more within.

Despite it all, I could still feel Cade. So close and real.

Magic flared around him as he shifted back to his human form. He stood right next to me, his heat still reaching for me. I looked up, struck anew by how tall and broad he was. His pupils were blown out, darkening his eyes, which roved over my face.

Electricity prickled between us.

He'd felt it, too, that same intimacy I'd sensed.

I sucked in a ragged breath, resisting the urge to lean up and press a kiss to his strong jaw. Or his full lips.

Out the corner of my eye, I spotted his hands turning to fists. He drew in a slow, steady breath, then stepped back. Tension sparked in the air between us, remnants of one of the most intimate supernatural acts.

CHAPTER SEVEN

"Come on." Cade's voice was rough. "We should get inside before anyone sees us."

"Yeah. Definitely." I looked away from him, up at the city towering above. There were at least a dozen buildings stacked on top of each other, all made of pressed sand with several walkways and tunnels weaving through them.

The exterior was rough and worn, though it looked like it'd once been carved with decorative leaves and flowers. Now, it was crumbling and pockmarked with gray streaks. From the VDBs, or the dark curse?

All the same, it was truly fantastical. Something straight out of another world.

"This way." Cade led me toward an opening at the base of the wall.

It looked like it had once been wider, spilling out onto the desert plain, but it was boarded up with wood now. There was just a narrow opening for a regular-sized person to fit through. No giant VDBs.

I ran my hand over the rough wood as I stepped between the boards. "This was added later, wasn't it? After the VDBs arrived."

"I think so," Cade said.

I inspected the alley we'd entered. It was about ten feet across and lit by glowing yellow lamps. They weren't electric or fire, but magic.

This whole place probably didn't have electricity—the Fae were known for scorning modern conveniences. And when this place had reached its heyday a few hundred years ago, electricity hadn't even been invented.

I looked upward. This alley rose all the way up—a full six stories—and terminated at a wooden roof. Light streamed through cracks, shining on dust motes that danced in the air.

"Yeah, they added all the wood to keep out the VDBs." I shuddered. "Can't blame 'em."

"Why don't we see if we can find a bar or pub where we can ask around for information."

"Great idea."

We set off down the dark, narrow road. The buildings on either side looked abandoned, but noise came from higher up on our right.

A set of winding stairs caught my eye. "Come on."

I gestured for Cade to follow, then climbed onto the sandstone stairs.

As I climbed up into the city, it became clear there truly was no rhyme or reason to how the rooms and buildings had been laid out. Pathways cut through at all angles and heights, along with more stairs going up, down, left, and right.

Generally, it was dimly lit—especially in the alleys that had sandstone for a roof instead of slats of wood.

"This place is a trip," I muttered.

"Earth Fae used to live here," Cade said. "They could navigate this type of structure easily."

"I'm barely keeping my bearings. This must be why Jude's map is so sparse."

"There's never been much record of this place. I'd only ever heard of it. The maze city in the desert."

Pounding footsteps made me freeze. Behind me, Cade did the same. The hair on my arms rose as the footsteps came nearer.

Friend or foe?

"Oy! You there!" the voice sounded from my left.

I turned, searching the dimly lit passage.

A large man hurried toward us, hand raised. "What do you think yer doing?"

Foe.

"Run," I whispered. I'd seen this sort of man before. Big, gruff, voice full of command.

He was either police, or he liked to act like it.

And he was hunting for trouble.

I sprinted up the stairs, calculating that we were roughly three stories up. Cade stayed close behind, his footsteps silent.

At the next landing, I darted left, running down a darkened corridor and taking the next stairs on the right. We passed by windows lit with pale yellow light and two older women sitting in a doorway. Up and down, left and right, I ran through the maze.

Finally, I stopped, panting. We were at a crossroads, with two of the nearby buildings spilling yellow light into the passage.

"We lost them." Cade peered back down the way we'd come.

"Yeah."

"How'd you know he was trouble?" Cade asked.

I shrugged. "Got a sense for it, that's all. Didn't you hear it in his voice?"

"He was trying to indicate who was boss." Cade shrugged.

"Ha. Well, to someone of my size, that means *stay away*." I looked him up and down, taking in the muscles and magic. "But I bet no one pulls that trick with you. Not when they get up close."

"Not usually."

"Hmm. Well, stick with me, buddy. I'll show you the ones to

avoid." I might have some badass magic, but my desire to keep on the down-low had taught me how to stay away from trouble.

If there was going to be trouble, I wanted to be the one starting it.

The sound of music filtered down one of the streets. I tilted my head, trying to get a better sense of it.

"Hear that?" I murmured.

"Some kind of bar."

"Let's go find it." I set off after the music, walking down the abandoned street.

Yellow lamps lit our way. On either side of the road, there were apartments or houses or shops. I couldn't tell which, since the window glass was frosted and only allowed light to escape. For every set of lit windows, there were at least ten darkened ones. This place was definitely down and out.

"Just outcasts and outlaws living here now," Cade murmured. "Only the sorts willing to live with the VDBs."

I was all too familiar with that. Back in Death Valley, there was an underground mountain city called Hider's Haven. Ana and I had delivered outlaws to the city so they could hide out from whatever hunted them.

But we'd never wanted to live there ourselves—no matter what hunted us or how close it got.

I loathed this type of closed-in living. This was barely tolerable, and only because it was above ground.

Music spilled out of a doorway up ahead.

I sidled up to it and glanced inside, spotting a bar or night-club. The walls were covered in glittering green leaves—magic, not real leaves. Glasses of neon liquid in all the shades of the rainbow sat on blue glass tables, around which sat surly-looking individuals. Most of them had the dusty tan skin of the Earth Fae. Their hair were all shades of browns, as were their eyes. There were a few other species here and there, though I couldn't identify most of them.

On the tiny stage in the corner stood a woman with blue skin and fabulous wings, belting her heart out to some tune about Vampire Demon Bats stealing the one she loved.

I glanced at Cade. "Ready?"

"Let's go."

We entered and wound our way through the crowd, headed toward the blue-glass bar. Several people shot us suspicious looks, but I averted my gaze.

No doubt they weren't used to new people. It was going to be tricky to find someone to talk to about the dark curse hanging over this place.

We found an empty spot at the bar, and I eyed the many bottles of jewel-toned liquor. They were right up my alley—I didn't need to taste them to know I'd like them—but now wasn't the time to get tipsy.

I leaned my back against the bar and surveyed the room for potential targets. There was a group of women giggling at the end of the bar. Nope. A rowdy crowd of guys around a card table. Nope again. A drunken couple in the corner who were sucking on each other's faces. *Definitely* nope.

But that left a few loners hanging out around the place—men and women both.

"What do you say we split up?" I asked.

"And try our wiles separately?"

A grin tugged at the corner of my mouth. "I'd like to see your wiles."

His brows rose.

Whoops. I'd meant that to be a silly joke, but it was actually a *bit* too honest.

"Whatever," I said. "Just split up. Try to find something about the cause of this dark curse that's seeping into the Protectorate, then we'll reconvene."

"Good plan."

I watched him amble off toward a woman who sat alone near

the stage. She had a red bouffant and a dress that was seriously flattering on her curvy figure.

I didn't love the tug of jealousy, so I turned from them, scouting the end of the bar that wasn't staked out by the supernatural hen party.

And it looked like my luck was about to pan out.

A youngish guy was approaching me. Barely twenty, if I had to guess, with a skinny frame and a peacock's flare of blue hair. He was cute, if you were into teenagers.

My gaze strayed back to Cade, who now sat next to the pretty woman.

Yeah, I wasn't into teenagers.

But I pasted a welcoming smile onto my face and tried to make my eyes twinkle at the would-be suitor. From his faltering step, it probably came off as a bit manic.

I cleared my throat and toned it down, leaning against the bar in what I hoped was a seductive pose. When I started to keel over a bit too much, I stiffened and straightened.

Yeah, intentional flirting was not for me.

The kid stopped by my side, a few inches taller than me. "Hey, I haven't seen you around here before."

"Not my usual place." I tried a smile.

He didn't wince or back up, so it must have looked pretty normal. *Jackpot.*

This undercover stuff wasn't so hard. The Academy would be proud of me.

A slender female bartender approached us, her small horns peeking out from her black hair. A demon. Though what kind, I had no idea.

"What can I get you?" she asked.

"I have no idea." And it was true. I didn't recognize a thing on the menu above the bar.

"Try a Fae Fancy. My treat," the kid said.

"Is it pink?" I asked.

"Sure is." The bartender grinned, revealing four sets of fangs. She turned and went to make the drink.

I turned to the kid. "How'd you know I like pink drinks?"

He shrugged. "Don't most girls?"

Well, no. But I didn't correct him. I smiled instead, though it was more like baring my teeth. "I'm Bree."

"Emrys."

"Nice to meet you, Emrys."

The bartender returned with the Fae Fancy, and I took a sip while Emrys paid. The flavor of raspberries and the bite of liquor exploded on my tongue.

I grinned. "It's great."

"Good." He smiled.

Should I just jump into the questions or flirt a bit more? I was about to lead in with a comment about the weather—super exciting!—when a gruff voice sounded from behind us.

"I think this pretty lady wants a real man."

Ew.

I turned. The man who stood behind me was a hulking bruiser of a guy. A couple inches over six feet with muscles stacked on top of muscles and not much neck to speak of.

Call me crazy, but I was partial to necks.

"I know what I want." And it wasn't this dude.

"You're not from around here." The man leaned closer, giving me a whiff of way too much cologne. "Don't normally like outsiders. Except you, pretty girl."

"Ugh. Not my style." I conjured a dagger and pressed it lightly against his side. "Now, why don't you leave us alone?"

The kid stepped in between me and the bruiser. "Lay off the lady, huh?"

Not good.

The hulk pulled back a fist and punched Emrys in the stomach. He dropped his drink, which splattered cold blue stuff all over my pants, and doubled over.

I didn't actually want to stab the guy, so I threw a punch, nailing him in the face. He was so big he hardly moved, but his head snapped to the side.

A growl rose in his throat.

Fear and excitement rushed through me, like my body was a crowd of high schoolers screaming *"fight!"*

He turned to me, eyes flaring in rage, and raised a hand, his palm open.

He wanted to *slap* me?

It was almost an insult.

But Cade was there a half second later, yanking on the man's hand.

"Thanks." I threw another punch, this time giving it my all.

The guy swung to the side, and Cade shoved him to the ground. It all happened in a second.

Cade grinned at me. "Nice work."

"Yeah." We were a good team.

Emrys straightened, coughing. His wide gaze went to the jerk who was climbing up off the floor. Then he glanced around the bar. His face whitened.

I turned to look.

Everyone was getting to their feet—and worse, their faces were shifting. The pretty, human visages were transforming into haggard, feral faces with long fangs.

"Aw hell," Emrys muttered. "Fae fight."

"What's that?" I called on my magic, getting ready to blast the crap out of anyone who came near. Not that it would be a good idea, considering the fact that I could take down the city around us. Maybe I should stick to my sword.

The angry Fae started toward us.

"Outsiders shouldn't start fights," the bartender muttered.

Yeah, she had a point there.

"Come on," Emrys said.

Then he turned and ran.

I glanced at Cade, who nodded. Yep—a man after my own heart. I sprinted after Emrys, following him around the left side of the bar and out the back door. Cade brought up the rear.

The back alley was narrower than others we'd traversed. Emrys was already fifteen feet away, racing down the passage.

He looked back over his shoulder. "Hurry up!"

This wasn't how I'd expected to find an ally and hopefully get my answers, but I wasn't going to look a gift Fae in the mouth.

I picked up the pace, lungs burning.

Shouts sounded from behind us as the mob spilled out into the alley.

Cade and I followed Emrys left, up some stairs, and then right, along another alley.

It was a dead end.

Emrys crouched on the ground, fumbling with something. He looked up, eyes wild. "Hold them off! The trap door is stuck."

I spun. Cade did the same, standing between me and the mob. I joined him, calling my daggers from the ether.

Our would-be attackers spilled into the passage, haggard faces lit by the golden light of the wall lamps. They looked ravenous, their jaws hanging low to reveal fangs and their eyes burning bright.

"Shit, the Fae are scary," I murmured.

"In fighting form, yes."

One darted forward, claws outstretched. I chucked a dagger, aiming to maim, not kill. The dagger sank into the figure's side, and he shrieked, going to his knees and sprawling on the ground.

I threw my other dagger, taking out the Fae behind that one.

Magic swirled around Cade as he called his shield from the ether. He hurled it in a tightly controlled manner, bowling over a half dozen Fae before the shield returned to him like a bullet.

He caught like it was nothing.

"Almost there!" Emrys said.

Whatever he was doing, I hoped it got us out of here, because there were a *lot* of Fae. They just kept coming, climbing over the bodies of their fallen peers.

Oddly enough, their magic smelled mostly of fresh air and wide-open spaces on the prairie. They weren't evil—just *mad.* Or hungry?

"Back off!" a voice roared.

"Oh, shit." Emrys's voice went high with fear.

A figure in a long brown coat cut through the Fae who were now only twenty feet away. His magic rolled out in front of him like rancid black smoke.

The Fae might not feel evil, but this guy sure did.

"Don't get hit with his magic!" Emrys cried.

The evil Fae's face was as ragged as the rest, but his eyes burned with a particularly dark light. He raised his hand and threw a blast of smoky yellow magic at us.

Cade lunged in front of me and raised his shield, taking the brunt of the hit. The smoky yellow magic turned to liquid when it hit the metal. It splashed, and I lunged backward, avoiding it. Cade winced, something I'd never seen him do.

"We're through!" Emrys cried.

I spun, catching sight of him dropping through a trap door.

I had no idea where we were going, but it really didn't matter. The Fae were nearly on us.

I leapt into the dark hole. Cade followed.

Emrys lunged for the trap door and slammed it shut, then smashed his hand against an amber crystal that glowed in the wall. Magic surged on the air, glowing with a golden light that surrounded the trap door.

"It's locked." Emrys leaned against the wall of the dark tunnel, panting. His face was pale and sweaty.

Shakily, I joined Cade and leaned against the other wall, my muscles trembling. I hadn't realized how scared I was, but it hit me now. "What the hell was that?"

"We Fae are a little weird after being cooped up here so long."

Emrys pushed his hair off his sweaty forehead. "It's like cabin fever, but worse."

"You're one of them?" I asked. "Why didn't you turn?"

"I was the prey." He shrugged. "Happens to all of us at some point. Fights ignite our feral instincts. We shift into our battle form, consumed by bloodlust. But the one who's being chased usually stays sane—the ol' fight or flight instinct. We need to flee, because we won't win the fight."

"So, you would've shifted like they did if someone else was prey?"

"Basically." He gestured around. "It's why we built these escape tunnels. We don't want to kill each other, so we've had to think of clever ways around it."

I inspected the dark tunnel—it wasn't dissimilar from the rest of the passages around town, except for the fact it wasn't as well lit.

My gaze landed on Cade, who'd been unusually silent next to me. His shield was eaten through by the yellow liquid, which now gleamed on his skin. He was doubled over, his face pale and drawn.

"Oooh, shit," Emrys said. "He hit you?"

"What is that stuff?" I demanded.

"Deadly. The guy in the coat was The Pennaeth. The most powerful of us all. His magic is more deadly than anything in the world. Some kind of poison."

"There's no antidote?" Cade's voice was rough.

"I thought you could heal yourself?" I demanded, fear chilling my skin.

"Not this time." Cade winced. "I don't know why it's not working."

"Nothing can defeat the Bossan's magic," Emrys said. "It's the concentrated dark influence of the Fae."

"That sounds bad." My gaze raced over Cade.

"It is." Emrys pushed away from the wall and gestured for us to follow. "Come on. I can make you more comfortable, at least. My grandfather is a healer who can help."

We followed. I tried to put an arm around Cade to help him walk, but he shook his head.

"Don't let it touch you," he murmured.

Helplessness welled within me, making me feel like a rat trapped in a box.

"How long do I have?" Cade asked.

"You won't die—at least not from the poison." Emrys turned a corner and led us down a narrow passage. "But you won't get any better, either. Most people just kill themselves. The pain is too much to bear."

Oh, shit. Bile rose in my throat. I could almost imagine what Cade felt. As if I felt it myself. It was a weird kind of connection I'd never felt before.

"We need to get you back to the Protectorate," I said. "They'll have a cure."

"No, they won't," Emrys said.

I wanted to punch him.

"We need to finish this," Cade said. "It's vital that we find what's threatening the Protectorate."

"We're here." Emrys stopped in front of a ladder. "My place is up there. My grandfather will have something to help you with the pain."

We followed him up the ladder and onto a main street. The golden lamps glowed in this part of the Fae city, and several of the windows were lit from within. There were no feral Fae to be seen.

Emrys let us into the apartment, which had a relatively large living room decorated with old furniture. Doors led off from each wall, but I couldn't see into them. Emrys pointed to the couch. "You can wait there."

Cade limped over to the couch. I joined him, my stomach turning with worry.

"How do you feel?" I demanded.

"Fine." His voice was tight.

"Liar." I inspected the gleaming yellow liquid that coated his arm and was splashed across his chest in little droplets. "You really can't heal yourself?"

He shook his head, face pale. "This hasn't happened before."

Something that could take down a god? Dread opened a chasm in my chest. It made me feel hollow.

My gaze returned to his arm. Something in my chest tugged, an unfamiliar sensation of pain and knowledge. *Connection.*

Like I, too, was wounded.

Emrys returned to the room. "Come on. Grandfather has drawn a healing bath. It'll make you feel a little better, at least."

Cade rose, and I followed, twisting my hands. Emrys led us down a hall to another room. There was a shower in one corner, and a basin dug into the ground in the center of the room. Opaque, blue water filled the basin, steaming in the cool air.

Emrys pointed to the shower. "Wash the poison off in there, then get in the bath for thirty minutes. It should help some."

Cade nodded, then limped to the shower. I stood, helpless.

"You sure you want to be here for this?" Emrys asked.

"I'll turn around."

Emrys shrugged. "Up to you. My grandfather will come in a while and see if he can help more."

He turned to leave, but I reached out a hand to stop him. "Why are you helping us?"

"Isn't that what you came here for?" He smiled. "It's obvious now that you're not a trader or explorer."

"Yeah, but at most I expected some answers. Not this."

He shrugged. "Well, I'm not going to leave you to die, am I?"

I smiled. "Thank you."

He nodded and left. Cade was stripping out of his shirt, so I faced the wall.

He was so quiet—so drawn in by his pain. Did he even realize I was here?

Maybe not.

The water turned on. A low groan sounded. Images flashed through my mind. Cade in the shower. Naked. Cade hurt.

In pain.

That last one made my stomach turn.

A few minutes later, the water stopped running. I couldn't hear him, but I swore I could feel him walking across the room toward the bath. The water splashed slightly.

"I'm in," he said. "And decent."

I turned. He was submerged up to the middle of his chest in the milky, blue water. Broad muscles gleamed through the steam. I joined him, sitting on the ground.

"How do you feel?"

"Fine."

"Liar."

"Like I've been hit by a truck, then."

I'd wanted honesty, but I didn't like hearing that.

My gaze traced over the muscles of his chest, seeking damage from the poison. I saw nothing, but was drawn to the area nonetheless. A couple inches below his right collarbone, an area seemed to glow.

I pointed to it, careful not to touch his skin. "Did it hit you there?"

"Aye. How can you tell? There's no mark."

"I have no idea." His arm called to me—as if it, too, were shining with light. "And your left forearm. The poison covered half of it, didn't it? There are a few splashes on the back of it, too. And some in the middle of your chest."

"Are you really that observant?" he asked.

"No." I generally only noticed things that flew right at my face. Not little stuff like this. But somehow I just *knew* that was where the poison had been.

It called to me, urging me to touch his skin where it had landed. I could feel his pain on my own skin. I shifted on the hard ground, weirded out and uncomfortable.

Touch him.

The voice echoed in my head—feminine and unfamiliar.

Heal him.

Whoa!

I blinked. Was I hearing this right?

Magic sparked within me—something totally new. It filled me, ready to explode free.

Heal him. Use your gift.

The magic pulsed inside me, fighting to be set free—to be released into Cade. To heal him.

Holy fates—this was what had happened back at San Zaccaria in Venice, when I'd gained my new power over water.

Something was changing within me. More magic—new magic —swelled within my chest. Trying to break free.

Instinct drove me to press my hands to Cade's chest. He was hard and warm. On fire.

He flinched, surprised. His gaze rose to my own. A connection flared between us as I fed my magic into him, giving him a healing light that flowed from my chest, down my arms, and into him.

He gasped quietly, lips parting. Confusion creased his brow.

"What are you doing?" he murmured.

"No idea." My gaze raced over him, looking for signs of improvement.

In my head, the voice whispered, *More! More! Heal him.*

I followed its command, feeding him more magic.

"The pain is fading," he murmured. "How?"

"Still no idea." My breath grew short as the last of my magic flowed into him. I sagged, barely able to prop myself up against the hard ground.

Cade surged upright, the water sloshing, and reached for me.

His strong arms held me upright, keeping me from collapsing on the ground. Warmth flowed into me, tension and pleasure. Despite my exhaustion—and confusion and fear—my body heated, drawn to Cade.

I looked up at him, suddenly aware of his nakedness. Of the miles of muscles that were pressed against me. Of his closeness.

My breath caught, heat racing across my skin as visions of him kissing me raced through my head.

Then a voice came from the door to the room, jerking me out of my trance. "Eir."

CHAPTER EIGHT

I looked over. An old man stood in the doorway, his gaze riveted on me. Not to the giant naked god who was holding me—but on *me*.

"Air," he murmured, shaking his head. He made a symbol with his hands—something like making the sign of the cross, but a Fae version, I assumed. Then backed out of the room.

"What the hell?" I scrambled away from Cade and stood.

He sank back into the water, concealing himself. "You healed me."

"Did I?" I *thought* I had, but honestly, this whole thing was a mind scrambler.

"You did. I feel totally better." Awe lightened his features.

Emrys hurried into the room, his face creased with confusion and a tray of sandwiches in his hands. "What happened? Grandfather said he'd seen a ghost and went to his room."

"I have no idea," I said. "Can I speak to him?"

I wanted to know why he'd said *Eir*. What did that mean? Had he been talking to *me*?

"He'll have returned to his trance," Emrys said. "He spends

most of his time in meditation. Once he's in that state, he can't be woken."

Crap. "Do you know why he would have said *Eir?*"

Emrys shook his head. "No idea." His gaze moved to Cade. "You look a lot better, man."

Cade nodded but didn't say anything about me healing him. I kept my mouth shut, too. I didn't know what the hell was happening to my new magic, but I wasn't about to share it around.

As soon as we returned to the Protectorate, I was going straight to the library to look up Eir. And Rán. And Njord. I needed answers—and I needed them *now.*

Exhaustion hit me, making me sway. Actually, what I needed now was a shower and a nap. Using up all my magic to heal Cade had left me wobbly.

"We've got a spare room you can sleep in," Emrys said. "Just one bed, though."

He looked a bit sad, as if realizing his dream of picking me up was fading. Ah, well. There were more girls where I came from.

"I'll see you in the morning," Emrys said. "We can talk about why you're here then."

"Thanks," I said. "Do you mind if I shower?"

"All yours. Room is the one at the end of the hall on the left."

"Thank you." And boy, did I mean it. "Without you, we'd be screwed."

He nodded, then put the sandwiches on the counter near the door. "Here's some food if you want it. Night."

"Thank you," Cade said.

I turned to face the wall, away from Cade. "I'll give you a few minutes."

"Thanks." The water splashed, and this time, since he was healthy again, I could really imagine what he looked like without feeling guilty. Tall and muscled and *naked.*

I squeezed my eyes shut and pinched the bridge of my nose. I really needed to get a hold of myself.

We worked together, for fate's sake. Like, really worked together—on cases and everything.

Total conflict of interest, just like he'd said.

"I'm out," he said.

I just nodded, trying to get my breathing under control. A moment later, I turned around. He was gone.

Whew.

It didn't take me long to strip down and take a quick shower. The hot water pounded away at my sore muscles, feeling like heaven. I had no idea how this ancient desert town managed their plumbing, but right now, I really didn't care.

Once I was clean, I hopped out of the shower and scrubbed off with the thin green cloth that hung on the wall, then scarfed down some of the strange sandwiches that were filled with meat I definitely didn't recognize. Not PB&J, my fave, but I'd eat anything right now.

I found the bedroom at the end of the hall where Cade and I would spend the night.

It was dark inside, with no windows and only a low-burning candle on the bedside table. Cade was a lump under the covers on the far side of the bed, still as a log.

I had no idea if he was asleep, but I wouldn't put it past him to fake it. It was what I'd do if I'd come in here first.

As quiet as I could, I toed off my boots and blew out the candle, then slipped into bed next to him, climbing under the covers. The chill in the air was a marked contrast to Cade's heat from the other side of the bed.

I lay silent and stiff, tension vibrating through every muscle. There were only inches between us, a tiny space that buzzed with energy. All sorts of thoughts—sexy ones that I'd just *die* if he could read—raced through my mind.

Ages passed as I stared blindly at the ceiling, until finally, exhaustion pulled me deep into slumber.

~

Terror raced through my veins like acid, and my lungs burned as I ran through the quiet streets of Death Valley Junction.

"Rowan!" I yelled. "This isn't funny!"

I squinted down a darkened alley that was lit only by moonlight. A tumbleweed rolled past, but no Rowan.

"Rowan!" Fear and anger vibrated in my voice.

"I don't think she's hiding." Terror laced Ana's words. She ran at my side, hunting for our sister. We hadn't seen Rowan in hours, ever since she'd gone out to the truck at the side of the house.

"Where the hell could she be though?" In truth, I was terrified of the answer.

Ana stopped, panting. I stopped, too, my heart thundering, and turned to her.

Ana's blonde hair was done up in a mohawk, and heavy black makeup marked her eyes. She'd started wearing the style a year ago on her seventeenth birthday. Tears streaked down through the black eye paint.

"I think they got her." Ana's voice broke.

They. The shadowy figures who'd driven us from our home when we were children. Our mother had taken us and run, and we'd managed to stay hidden for over a decade.

Until now.

"But why would they take just her?" I asked. "If they managed to find us despite our concealment charms, why only take her?"

"I don't know."

I spun in a circle, the night heat pressing down on me. The streets of Death Valley Junction were empty. We'd spent the last two hours combing all the bars and alleys, but we'd had no luck.

"I can't believe she's gone," I said. We'd had no trouble since we'd moved here four years ago after our mother's death. And now?

Rowan was gone.

My heart tore in two as the reality sank in. My sister. Gone. Taken by those who hunted us.

~

I woke, a cry strangling in my throat. Wet tears streaked down my temples and into my hair.

Warm arms—*strong* arms—wrapped around me. Comforting. Constraining.

I thrashed, breaking free.

"Are you all right?" Worry edged Cade's voice.

I blinked, my vision returning. We were in bed together—the tiny one in the Fae apartment, I realized. I scrambled to sit upright, my heart pounding and tears still rolling down my cheeks.

Cade sat next to me, worry on his face. "What is it?"

I sucked in a ragged breath, trying to stop the tears long enough to talk. It was that awful, gasping kind of moment where you can't get a word out.

Cade opened his arms just enough to be an invitation. I gave in, falling into his arms and weeping, and pain tore through my chest. I hadn't dreamt of Rowan's disappearance in years. And it'd felt like I was back there—reliving it.

After a while, the dream faded, along with the grief. Embarrassment was quick to rush into its place.

We were colleagues, not in a relationship. And all I'd done was lust after Cade or cry on him.

I wanted to be cool and collected, not a mess of emotion.

But there was no denying it—I was one big mess. Of emotion, magic. A disaster.

"What's wrong?" Cade asked.

I scrubbed my hands over my face to get rid of the tears. "Nothing."

"Aye, Bree. That looks like nothing." He squeezed my shoulder, then dropped his hand. His expression was pure acceptance. No judgment.

I sighed, my breath ragged. "I dreamed about the time my sister went missing."

"You mentioned her before."

"It's pretty much the defining moment of my life. And Ana's. We want to find her."

"Understandable." His gaze turned serious. "When this is over, it will be our priority to find her."

"Thank you." Hope flared in my chest. He'd offered to help before, but I was glad we were moving up the timeline. I couldn't bear to wait anymore. Even if I hadn't proved myself to the Protectorate yet, I wanted their help finding Rowan as much as I hated accepting it.

Taking help from anyone for any reason had always rubbed me wrong—but Ana and I had already tried everything we could to locate Rowan.

If she was even still alive.

I shook away the horrible thought, unwilling to go there. Positivity was the only way forward. Action, above all else.

And if I was going to find Rowan, I needed to save the Protectorate. It was my home now. And it was my best shot at finding Rowan.

"We'll find her, Bree," Cade repeated.

Warmth filled me. It was a light of hope and gratitude and joy and just sheer *liking* Cade. Our time together—as fraught with danger as it'd been—had proven to me that I liked him. I wasn't just attracted to him. It was more than that.

And I needed to shove it down deep and focus on the task at hand.

I climbed out of bed, breaking the spell of intimacy with Cade. "Let's get going. I feel like we're getting close to answers."

Cade nodded and climbed out of bed. We pulled on our shoes and left the room, following a savory smell.

Emrys was inside a kitchen, pulling a kettle off the stove. The space was more rustic than the kitchens I was used to, but the food on the table was obviously breakfast.

"You sleep all right?" Emrys asked.

"Aye, thank you," Cade said.

We sat.

Emrys gestured to the food, which looked like some kind of porridge. "Help yourself."

I filled a heaping bowl and dug in. The porridge tasted a bit like savory leaves—which was pretty freaking weird—but I was so hungry that it was good anyway.

Emrys took the chair across from us. "So, what brings you here? Clearly, you're after something."

I nodded, swallowing. "The dark curse that's spreading over this realm. What is it?"

"No idea. It started a week ago and has been getting worse every day."

Only a week?!

"Worse?" Cade asked.

"Yep." Emrys pointed to the wall. "It's crumbling more than it was before. It's the curse's fault. And people have been more irritable the last week—more than usual. I think it's one of the reasons they attacked so quickly last night. Normally, it'd take more than that to get them to shift into their fighting form."

Shit. This was what would happen to the Protectorate if the curse spread. "So it's like a destruction curse of some kind?"

"I think so."

"Why isn't anyone doing anything about it?" Cade asked.

"The source of the curse is coming from the abandoned village of Eidollawn. No one is willing to go there, except me."

"Why? What's there?"

"Nothing except the VDBs. They took it as their main roost when they invaded hundreds of years ago. There are thousands there." Sadness glinted in his blue eyes. "When the VDB arrived, most of our people left, going to another realm. Those of us that refused to go—or weren't allowed to, because we were locked in the jail—stick to this village. No one—and I mean *no one*—goes to Eidollawn. Except me."

"Why do you go?" Cade asked.

"Scavenging. There aren't a lot of ways to make a living here, and I don't want to join a gang." He shrugged. "A few years ago, I found tunnels into Eidollawn. I sneak through the houses and take things I can sell. It's not like those people need it anyway. They're long dead and gone."

"You haven't tried to get other people to go to Eidollawn to stop the curse from spreading? And *how* does it come from there?"

"I *did* try to convince the Elders. But like I said, everyone is irritable. They weren't willing to listen. And there's a terrible taboo surrounding Eidollawn, anyway. They weren't willing to consider it. Until now, I haven't even told people it's where I get my goods."

"I can't believe the Elders won't do anything about it." I didn't know what a Fae Elder was, exactly. But the name *Elder* made me think of kindly guardians.

Emrys shrugged. "We've lived through terrible things before —they assume we'll live through this, too. But I'm not so sure."

"The curse spreads quickly," Cade said. "It's only been a week."

"Are you trying to imply that they could come around?" Emrys laughed. "Because I don't think so."

"It doesn't matter either way," Cade said. "We're here to stop it. Can you take us to the source of the curse?"

"Is it a person?" I asked.

"A portal," Emrys said.

A portal. Which meant that dark magic was coming from somewhere else, spreading through this land, and then through our portal into the Protectorate.

Were they targeting us on purpose? "Where does the portal go?"

"I have no idea," Emrys said. "It hasn't been there long. Only a couple weeks. I never had the guts to go into it."

"Can't blame you," I said.

"The portal is coming from a well in the center of Eidollawn. I took the information to the Elders and struck out."

"And you went to the bar after," I said.

"What better place to drink my sorrows?" He grinned, suddenly looking so young. "And it brought me to you two. The ones who will help. It's fate."

"Fate." I believed in fate. I *had* to believe in fate. I'd been a leaf blowing in the wind my whole life. The moment I got a bit of control—like over our life in Death Valley—was the moment that something went haywire.

So I had to believe in fate—that there was a reason all this crazy shit happened to me.

"Exactly," Emrys said. "I'll take you to Eidollawn. But I won't return to the portal."

"Why not?" Cade asked.

"Scary as hell, man." Emrys shook his head, his face pale. "Why do you think I hightailed it away from there and told the Elders? Then went to drink it away when they said they wouldn't help?"

"It's fine," I placated. I didn't want to lose Emrys. We needed him. "Can we go now?"

Emrys nodded and stood. "Yeah. My grandfather will sleep most of the day, so I can go. I just need to be back by nightfall to sit with him."

"All right." We'd run into a lot of considerate young men in this Fae world.

"Come on." Emrys led us out of the house.

We followed him down the narrow street toward the right. The city was quiet this early in the morning. Though it wasn't bright, sunlight gleamed through the cracks in the wooden roof, shining sharp rays of light on the street below.

We made our way down to the ground level at the far edge of town. We were on the other side of the town from where we'd entered, if my sense of direction was leading me right.

The scent of animals filled the streets here.

"I have a carriage," Emrys said.

Carriage? As in horse and...?

He led us into a large stable where strange Fae horses stamped their feet and whinnied.

Yep. Horse and carriage.

It made sense that they didn't have cars, since this place had pretty much frozen in time hundreds of years ago. Still, I wished we had the buggy.

Emrys was quick in gathering four horses—if one could call the horned, fanged creatures horses—and attaching them to a sleek-looking carriage.

I walked around the vehicle, appreciating its lines. The tires were large and sturdy, while the body was simple. Just a bench and cargo bed in the back.

"I bet this goes fast," I said.

"Sure does." Emrys patted the neck of the horse. "Built it myself just for this journey."

The horse turned to look at me, yellow eyes gleaming. The creature's hair looked like it was made of glittering amber, and its horns sparkled with golden light.

Emrys climbed up onto the seat. "Come on."

We climbed up next to him, and he snapped the reins. The four horses started trotting, their gait higher than that of a normal horse. We neared the large barn doors, and they swung open.

Morning sun blazed into the dimly lit barn, and Emrys grinned. "I don't know how people stay cooped up in there all the time. I'd go crazy if I didn't get out occasionally."

"You aren't worried about the VDBs?" Cade asked. "It can't be easy to drive and fight them off at the same time."

"Nah." Emrys shook his head. "My horses are fast, and the carriage is protected by a concealment charm. The VDBs can't see us in this."

"Handy," I said.

"Yep." Emrys frowned. "Though I'm a bit worried about the sand plains across the river. The increased weight of the carriage might wake the sand skeletons."

"We can fight them off," I said. "As long as there aren't hundreds."

Emrys made an unconvinced noise, as if there might actually *be* hundreds.

Despite Emrys's assurances that we were hidden from the VDBs, I stayed alert on the ride away from the Fae city. The land spread out in either direction, packed tan dirt that reminded me a bit of Death Valley, but without the insane heat. The sun was bright overhead, making it easy to spot any oncoming attacks, but there were none.

Yet.

"Almost to the river," Emrys said.

I could feel it inside my chest—a strange knowledge that we were close to a large body of water. What the heck *was* my new magic?

The roar of rapids hit my ears before I spotted the river. "Where is it?"

"Down low, in the gorge." Emrys directed the carriage closer.

As we neared, I realized the land dropped away in front of us. Stone bridges made from the earth itself arched over the gorge, bisecting and joining up with each other in a lattice of rock. There were dozens of them.

"It's a mile across," Emrys said. "Widest river in all the realms."

"No kidding." It felt like my whole body was suffused with the water. Like I was *one* with it. And there was a lot of it.

Emrys directed the carriage onto the first arched stone bridge. It was barely as wide as the vehicle, and the drop was thousands of feet to the river below. I leaned over and looked down, spotting the water rushing by, slowly carving away at the rock posts that supported the arched bridge.

The horses were quick as they crossed this section of rock and moved onto the next, as if they'd come this way dozens of times before.

"These are natural rock formations?" I asked. They were fabulous—ornate and delicate. A true fairy land.

"Yeah. Really old, too." Emrys directed the horses onto the last stretch of bridge.

My shoulders relaxed when we arrived on the other side. Solid ground felt good, no matter how much control I had over water.

"Yah!" Emrys sped the horses along.

They picked up the pace, galloping across the dirt toward a massive forest ahead of us.

"Be on the alert," Emrys said. "This is where the sand skeletons dwell. They normally leave me alone, but with your weight on the carriage, they might wake."

Please don't wake. I'd had enough of skeletons in Venice.

I peered around, ready for an attack. Next to me, Cade was alert and ready.

Nerves tightened my muscles. I *loathed* waiting. Would they attack? Wouldn't they?

Screw it.

Just attack already!

When the first rumbling in the ground made the carriage vibrate, I grinned savagely, relief flowing through me.

"The wait is over!" I spun around on the seat, searching.

Behind us, the ground shifted and caved slightly. Then a sand skeleton burst forth. It was easily fifteen feet tall and made of the packed dirt that formed the ground below. It was shaped roughly like a skeleton, but that was where the similarities ended.

More popped out of the dirt. Six in all. They charged, chasing after the carriages, their footsteps pounding the earth.

"Try your sonic boom!" Cade said. "Remember what we talked about."

I scrambled to my feet, climbing onto the back cargo platform of the carriage. This was pretty much like fighting from the buggy. I was in my element, and I liked it.

"Hurry up!" Emrys shouted. "If they catch us, they'll crush the carriage."

I called upon my magic, clearing my mind in the way Cade had taught me. Though I could feel my magic inside me, strong and fierce, I couldn't find my gift of the sonic boom. Normally, it felt distinct.

But now, I felt nothing.

The sand skeletons charged toward us, gaining by the second.

"Go on," Cade said. "It's not the time to dawdle."

"I'm not dawdling!" Frustration welled inside me as I tried to get a handle on my sonic boom.

It thrashed in my chest, flickering and faint. I grabbed hold of it, imagining a huge sonic boom, and hurled it out toward the sand skeletons.

Nothing happened.

"What's wrong?" Cade demanded.

I tried again, hurling my magic toward the skeletons.

Nothing.

My skin grew cold, fear lancing through me. This had never happened before. Sure, the boom might go haywire or be too weak, but it'd never *disappeared*.

I tried one last time, desperation fueling me. The sand skeletons were nearly to us. *Out of time.*

I hurled my sonic boom.

And nothing happened.

I wanted to scream.

Instead, I sucked in a ragged breath and called upon my new gift over water. Now wasn't the time to panic. The sand skeletons were only twenty feet away from swiping at us with their massive hands.

The water in the river called to me, connecting with my magic and my will. It was strange and foreign, but I went on instinct, envisioning the water rising up from the gorge and smashing the sand skeletons.

"Bree, do you need help?" Cade asked. His desire to leap into action vibrated on the air. The sand skeletons were *so* close.

"I got this!" I said, praying to fate that I really did.

I called to the water, using my new magic. It felt like manipulating putty with my mind. At first, it seemed like nothing was happening—that I was just going crazy.

But then the water rose up from the gorge behind us, a massive fist formed of glittering liquid. It reached out toward the sand skeletons, crushing them into the dirt like I'd imagined.

They turned to mud, washing away. Water splashed us.

"Holy fates." Cade's voice was low with awe.

"What the heck was that?" Emrys yelled.

"Nothing!" I said. "Just keep driving."

My mind buzzed with what had just happened, my breath coming quick. I kept my gaze glued on the terrain around us, praying there were no more sand skeletons. We were far enough from the water that I could feel my grip on it loosening.

I wasn't like Caro, who could create the water. I needed to be close to it to use it. But *boy*, could I use it.

"We're out of their territory!" Emrys finally yelled.

My muscles were still vibrating with tension as I returned to my seat. Cade was looking at me with some serious interest, his gaze glued to my face.

"What happened there?" he whispered at my ear, so quietly that Emrys wouldn't be able to hear over the rushing wind.

I shivered at the feel of his breath, but it was shock over what had just happened that loosened my tongue. "My sonic boom power is gone."

"Gone? That's not possible."

"Apparently it is." When had it happened? Just recently, since I'd used it only a day ago. "It wasn't there when I tried to call to it. And I can't feel it anymore."

"But you can control the water. You have more power than a hundred Water Mages."

I nodded, unable to deny what he'd just seen. A giant freaking fist made of water had reached thousands of feet up from the river to crush my opponents.

Holy crap.

Something was definitely happening to me. And it was freaking serious.

CHAPTER NINE

Thirty minutes later, we reached a steep mountain range. Emrys directed the carriage through a deep valley between the mountains. The horses galloped through the passage. On either side of us, the mountains rose high into the air.

Eventually, the passage ended, opening up to a grassy plain that stretched ahead of us.

"That's it up ahead," Emrys said. He pointed toward a grove of *massive* trees about three hundred yards away. Each one had to be a thousand feet tall. They put the redwoods to shame.

Awe filled me at the sight of them towering far overhead. Huge branches extended outward, each dotted with black specs.

"Are those black things the VDBs?"

Emrys nodded. "It's why they like that area so much. They don't care much for the town, which is in the middle of the grove, but they love the trees."

"How do you get across? Just hope that your spell will keep you concealed?"

"That might work, but normally I play it safe." He jumped off the carriage and tied it off to a large rock. "Come on, I'll show you."

Cade and I hopped down and followed Emrys to a break between two rocks. It was a skinny opening, but wide enough that we could fit. Barely.

Emrys pointed into it. "You'll go in there. It leads one way—straight into town. I think it used to be an escape route for the town in times of war, but now it's unused."

"You sure you won't come with?" I asked.

"No way in hell. Just be careful in the tunnel. It's lit by the glowing amber, but don't touch it. The pixies won't like it."

"Aye, we won't." Cade stuck out his hand. "Thanks, mate."

"Do you need a ride back?"

Cade shook his head. "This sounds like what we're looking for. Once we've done some recon, we can use a transport charm to get home."

"Good. Be safe. And don't let the VDBs see you. They're always hungry."

I nodded, shivering at the memory of their long fangs. "Thanks again, Emrys. And thanks for the drink at the bar."

"Good luck," he said. "You need anything to help with this, let me know. I want it gone from this realm."

"I don't blame you." I shook his hand, and he made quick work of leaving. I turned to Cade. "Ready?"

"More than. I'm ready to get out of this realm."

"Me too." The dangers here made Earth look like a kid's playground.

I followed Cade into the darkened tunnel, my eyes adjusting to the low light. As Emrys had said, veins of amber ran through the walls, glowing with a golden sheen. Pixies floated near the ceiling, shining with their own light. They were amazing.

"I've never seen anything like them. Normally, pixies don't like it underground."

"They feed on the amber." Cade set off down the tunnel.

I followed, my gaze tracing over the jagged rock and gleaming amber. The pixies floated around my head, tiny fairies that peered closely at me before darting away.

The air smelled dusty and dry, and the farther we got into the tunnel, the darker the amber grew. I peered at it, realizing the dark curse was staining the surface.

"It gets worse," I said.

"There's barely any glow up ahead," Cade said.

He was right. A hundred yards ahead, there were no more pixies and the amber was so muted that it was hard to see.

"Oh, this curse sucks." I shivered, horrified at the idea of this curse spreading far enough to break down the Fae city and eventually the Protectorate.

"We'll stop it."

I liked the certainty in Cade's voice.

Finally, we reached a larger opening. The room was entirely black, with only the slightest glow allowing me to see the ladder that rose up along one wall.

"That way." I pointed to it.

Cade, of course, managed to get to the ladder first and go up, but I was right behind him.

The stench of the curse—which I *thought* I'd become inured to —made my eyes water anew and my gag reflex act up. I swallowed hard and kept climbing, desperately trying to focus.

By the time I climbed through the trap door into the room above, my heart was thundering with anticipation and fear.

What would we find here?

The room that housed the trap door to the passage was small and nondescript. Piles of blackened wood rested against the walls, and a quick inspection revealed that it was furniture— destroyed by the curse.

"Holy fates." I stepped back, horror opening a chasm in my chest.

"Come on," Cade said. "We shouldn't spend long here."

"No kidding." I followed him to the door, which had

completely decayed away, and peered out into what had once been a central square in town.

A massive well sat in the middle of it, big enough to drive a bus into. All around, the buildings were black and decayed, crumbling on their foundations. The trees rose high above the town, the bottoms of their trunks blackened.

"I hope this doesn't kill the trees." I'd never seen anything so magnificent.

"It's doing us a small favor though." Cade pointed up. "No VDBs in those branches."

I squinted upward. He was right. They were bare. I stepped out of the doorway, ready to get this over with and check out the portal. "Come on."

We hurried across the square to the portal, which gleamed with the same oily black sheen as the one leading to the Protectorate's castle.

I stopped when I was still about fifteen feet away. This was more than close enough to see—and smell. The stench of rotten eggs was so strong that my eyes burned.

"This place feels haunted," Cade said.

"Agreed." I stared hard at the oily surface of the portal, trying to see through it to the other side. It was an impossible endeavor, but I was desperate. "Ready to go in?"

"Aye."

I climbed onto the low, stone wall that surrounded the well. Cade joined me. I held out a hand. He took it.

He counted down. "Three, two, one."

We jumped, plunging into cold, oily water.

Shit!

I hadn't realized it'd be *full.*

I called on my magic, forcing the water down through the well. We fell along with it, whooshing through the tunnel until the ether sucked us in, taking control.

It thrust us out onto hard ground. I stumbled, falling to my knees and barely stopping myself with my hands. Gravel cut into my palms.

I looked up. My skin crawled.

This was hell.

The sky was black, cut through by frequent lightning strikes, and thunder shook the earth. Far in the distance, a large building sat on a hill, surrounded by a wall.

The curse came from there. I could just feel it. The magic was so strong here that it made my insides feel tainted. Polluted.

Between us and the building were rows of protections. Massive monsters prowled just outside the building gates, an unidentifiable species from this distance. They looked tiny from here—but the fact that I could see them at all indicated how big they really were.

Then there were rows upon rows of thorny brambles. The spikes on the edges of the branches were at least a foot long, and I'd bet money the brambles could move, striking out at a person.

But closest to us were the same kinds of oily monsters that had attacked us at the other portal. They were tall and slim with elongated heads, and their skin was covered in shiny black oil that gleamed whenever the lightning struck.

As if on cue, they turned to us.

Then they charged.

I looked at Cade.

"We need reinforcements," Cade said.

"Yep!" I turned.

Together, we leapt back into the portal. This time, it easily sucked us through, spitting us back out in the Fae realm.

I'd never have thought this place felt safe, but life comes at you fast.

Panting, I turned to look at Cade. "I hate to run from a fight, but that was a good move."

"Aye. If we tried to cross that wasteland and failed, the Protectorate will fall. They won't have time to learn what we've learned.

We need to come back with something that will destroy this portal from the other side."

"And get us across that land so we can get some answers. Because whoever is sending that curse here—they're protecting themselves. They don't want us to stop them." I turned to study the oily surface of the portal, trying to see through it to the other side.

When the sleek, faceless figure pushed out of the black surface, reaching for me with a clawed hand, I jumped backward.

"Breeeee," it hissed. "Come to me."

"Oh, crap." My heart thundered.

But the figure couldn't escape—all it could do was reach for me and call out.

"Let's get the hell out of here," Cade said.

I hurried to him as he pulled a transport stone from his pocket. I grabbed his hand, and he hurled the stone to the ground. As I stepped into the cloud, the creature called my name again.

"Breeeeeee."

CHAPTER TEN

When we arrived back in the forest at the Protectorate, dread filled me. The trees were now covered with a blackened film, and the ground was entirely dark. The fairy lights that normally sparkled between the trees were faded and dim.

"Oh, no."

Cade grabbed my hand. "Come on."

I followed him, hurrying out of the forest. Halfway out, I realized I was still holding his hand. He seemed to notice at the same time, too. He loosened his grip. I pulled away and blushed.

Getting caught up in the stress of the moment was one thing —holding hands all the way out of the forest? Nope—not professional.

Especially since it heated my insides. Which just made guilt flare. This was *not* the time.

The sun was setting behind the mountains when we exited the forest, sending a golden glow over the massive castle and the mountains surrounding the exterior walls. The stone battlements nearest the forest were blackened with the curse, and even the castle itself was starting to turn a light gray.

"We're running out of time," I said.

"Aye, but we'll stop it."

I clung to his certainty as we ran across the lawn. I didn't want to lose my new home. Especially to a threat that might have something to do with me.

Breeeee, the monster had said. *My* name. Not Cade's or Hedy's or Jude's.

I swallowed hard, straightening my spine, and followed Cade through the massive wooden doors that swung open.

There was a somber air to the great hall. By all accounts, evening was party hour. The castle transformed from a work environment to a living environment—but not today.

People were hurrying up and down the stairs and across the hall, faces set and arms filled with books or weapons or magical amulets. Everyone was hard at work—probably trying to find a way to save the castle.

"You're back!" The excited voice made me look toward the stairs.

Caro was halfway down, her platinum hair gleaming in the light. Relief glinted in her eyes. "I'll alert the others."

"My sister, too," I said.

"We'll meet in the round room," Cade said.

Her face paled just slightly, and she nodded, then turned and ran back up the stairs.

"The round room?" I asked.

"The war room, I should have called it," he said. "It's where we meet when things are dire. Our presence there may help call Arach to us."

If anyone could fix this, it was the dragon spirit. But she so rarely showed up at the castle—I'd only met her the one time. She might not even show for this, though I certainly thought it was worth her time.

We hurried down the wide hall that was lined on either side with massive old paintings. Cade turned left, into a room that was circular. The stone walls were hung with tapestries, and the table within was massive and round—just like where the knights of old might have sat. It was the oldest room in the castle I'd ever seen, the walls made of ancient stone and the floor a beaten wood.

"I hope you've got an answer for us." Jude's voice made me turn.

She entered the room, her face creased and tired, and her braids pulled back.

"We have some answers," I said.

"Good." She took a seat at the far end of the table.

Hedy hurried in, her silver and lavender hair matching her flowing dress. She, too, looked tired, and gave us only a weary, hopeful smile. The other three department heads walked in. Potts —looking grumpy as ever—and the slender, pale woman who ran the Department of Interspecies Mediation. Kate Warrington, as I recalled.

"Is it demons?" Ammons, the third department head demanded. He was a big man, built like a football player, and he ran the Demon Trackers Unit.

"Maybe," I said, recalling the strange creature.

"Maybe?" he groused as he sat. "We'd hoped you'd have more than that."

I was saved from having to reply by Ana's entrance. "Thank fates you're okay."

She ran to me and threw her arms around me. Out the corner of my eye, I saw Cade go to sit next to Ammons, expertly drawing and then deflecting his attention.

I hugged Ana. "I'm fine."

Caro, Haris, and Ali brought up the rear. Jude nodded at them, then pointed to the chairs next to her. They worked for her department, the Paranormal Investigative Team. It was the one I hoped to join if I succeeded in my training, but it certainly wasn't a given. It was the most elite unit, by far. Cream of the crop.

The fact their acronym was the PITs belied the fact that they were immensely clever and talented.

Which was why they were here. And I was grateful for it. Given what we'd seen, we could use all the help we could get.

I sat next to Cade with Ana at my side. Nearly all the chairs were full, but the room was dead silent.

Everyone turned to look at us.

Jude spoke. "It's been getting worse. The wall near the forest is nearly crumbled, and the castle is at risk. Tell us you have good news."

Cade gestured to me. I blinked, briefly taken aback.

I was just a trainee.

But what had Jude said? This was a test. It was me, learning to think on the ground. Solve real-world problems and mysteries. Just like the PITs would do.

And that monster *had* called my name.

I sucked in a deep breath and described what we'd seen, starting with the abandoned Fae land, Rocky, the VDBs, and finally, the portal.

"*Another* portal?" Jude's face was stark. "That's not good."

"Someone is using the Fae realm to get to us," Ammons said. "Our external walls are too strong—especially since the reinforcements two weeks ago. So they're coming in through the abandoned Fae land. They can't get through the portal, but their curse can."

It was what I'd been afraid of. That Ana and I were somehow to blame. The timing was too much. Believing in coincidences was lazy and dangerous.

"That assumes they are targeting us," Hedy said. "We could just be collateral damage."

"Too risky to assume that," Jude said. "They called Bree's name. We need to attack this head-on. Assume they're coming for us and bring the fight to them. We *can't* let them breach the walls."

"I agree with Jude," Cade said. "We can fight a battle on our own turf, but the risk is too great. The armory is too valuable, and so is Hedy's magical stockpile. We can't let those things fall into the hands of outsiders."

"Don't forget the library," Potts said. "Millions of priceless spell books and history tomes."

Hope flared in my chest. Maybe they were just after all the goodies in the castle? This place *was* full of treasures.

Again—coincidence. Too convenient. Too good. And that monster had called my name. *My* name. This was connected to me.

"The good news is that the Fae boy Emrys said the portal is only a couple weeks old, correct?" Hedy asked.

"Yes." I nodded.

"That means I can close it. It's far easier to destroy younger portals than older portals."

"What we need is a two-prong attack," Cade said. "Someone to find out who is doing this, and someone else to close the portal."

"I want to go after them." I had to get into that building. Had to find out.

"She's just a trainee!" Potts crowed. "Recon is one thing. But the attack op? Unheard of!"

Jude's sharp gaze turned to me, considering.

"The monster called my name," I said. "I want to find out who's behind this."

Jude nodded. "It looks like we're advancing your training from recon to outright attack op."

"I want to help her," Ana said.

Jude frowned.

"We're best as a team," I added. "And I think we should bring the buggy. It's a long way through dangerous defenses to get to that building."

The directors all looked at each other, then turned to us.

"It could be destroyed," Hedy said. "Emily can transport it, but there's no guaranteeing it will make it back."

The idea made my chest ache, but I nodded. If this was a sacrifice I needed to make to protect my new home, I'd do it.

"Good," Hedy said. "If you can go through the portal to catch whoever is doing this, I can set up an explosive device to destroy the portal. That way we'll ensure the curse can no longer hurt us. It'll be dangerous, but it should do the job."

Whatever magic Hedy was going to deploy—it had to be something crazy. That was a huge portal.

"Then we have a plan," Jude said. "Cade, Bree, and Ana will go through the portal. Caro, Haris, and Ali will accompany them as backup. The rest of us will help Hedy with the destruction spell."

I nodded, satisfaction spreading through me. I wanted this finished, though I was dreading what I'd find. "I'm sorry if we brought this here."

Everyone turned to look at me. My face flamed.

"We don't know that," Jude said. "But we have your back. You're part of the team now."

I nodded, grateful. A weird kind of warmth bloomed in my chest. I'd only ever felt this kind of acceptance from my sisters and mother. The idea that there were more people out there—a whole organization—who might accept me was pretty freaking awesome.

"We'll start in the morning," Cade said. "Caro, if you'll handle getting more potions from Melusine that will allow other members of the Protectorate through the portal, that would be excellent."

Caro nodded. "On it. We'll hit her up tonight."

We finished our specific planning for the morning, then rose. Cade and I shared one look that lasted longer than necessary, then left the room, going in separate directions.

Ana joined me on the way up to our rooms.

"Are you all right?" She kept her voice low.

"Hungry, tired, totally freaked out."

"About as I'd expect."

We made our way through the winding halls toward our wing.

"What's the deal with Cade?" she asked as we reached an empty section of hallway. "I noticed that look you guys shared."

"The usual. Sexual tension out the wazoo, but we're denying it. It's the only smart thing to do."

"True that." She stopped at her door. "You want to grab a bite to eat—and definitely a shower—then meet me back here to go search the library?"

"Definitely." I hadn't yet told her about my changing magic, but she was reading my mind as usual. Didn't matter how tired I was—I wanted answers.

"Thirty minutes," she said.

I gave her a thumbs-up, then hurried up the stairs to my tower apartment. I'd only lived here a couple weeks, but I freaking loved my little place. I entered and flicked on the lights, the most amazing sense of *home* flowing through me.

The sight of the ghostly Pugs of Destruction made my jaw drop. "What the heck?"

As usual, Mayhem sat on the couch with half a ham in her mouth. That dog went nowhere without her ham.

Chaos sat in my clean laundry basket, the laundry up to his neck. He grinned, tongue lolling out and horns sticking up toward the sky.

But it was Ruckus who really caught my eye. The dog sat in my sink, which was full of water. His fangs glinted in the light.

"Are you taking a bath?"

He barked an obvious denial.

"There are bubbles in there."

He looked away.

"Whatever." I shut the door and went to the fridge, pulling out a leftover pizza we'd gotten in Edinburgh the day before I'd discovered the dark curse. I'd eaten all the PB&J in the house, as usual, and had to make do.

I opened the box and sniffed hesitantly. Smelled all right.

Three barks sounded.

The Pugs of Destruction surrounded me—even Mayhem with her ham in her mouth. They clearly thought the pizza was okay to eat.

I shoved a slice into my mouth and stared at their hopeful faces.

Pizza probably wasn't good for dogs. But these guys were freaking ghosts.

They barked again.

"All right, all right." I tossed them each a slice, which they caught in their mouths. Even Mayhem managed to catch hers without dropping her ham. "You guys really are magical."

I left them to enjoy the spoils of their victory and took a quick shower. I pulled on clean clothes. I'd favored a desert outlaw look back in Death Valley, with leather pants and strappy leather tops. Here in Scotland, I replaced the tops with a T-shirt and leather jacket. It might be late summer but I wasn't used to the chill.

All dressed, I left and headed over to Ana's apartment.

She wasn't downstairs yet, so I climbed the stairs and knocked on her door. She pulled it open, revealing the apartment behind her.

Since each apartment magically decorated itself according to the tastes of its owner, hers looked entirely different from mine. It was a more classic style—lots of whites and creams but with crazy colorful paintings on the old stone walls.

"Ready?" I asked.

"Yep."

We hurried back down the stairs, and Ana took the lead. "I found the library while you were gone. But Potts doesn't like me. So it's better we're going at night."

"I'm not sure Potts likes anyone."

She chuckled. "True."

The sound of dog nails clicking on the wooden floor sounded from behind us. I turned. The Pugs of Destruction trotted along behind us. Mayhem's ham was just a bone now, but she had it gripped fiercely between her teeth.

"Seriously, guys, you're going to have to be quiet," I said. "We're going to the library."

They woofed low.

"They have a great respect for the library, actually," Ana said. "They accompanied me the first time. Potts actually liked them."

Maybe Potts wasn't so bad.

Ana led me through the darkened halls of the castle. This place was so big that I'd never get to know it all. Every day, it seemed like there was a new hallway or room. And no two were alike. It was as if this place had been built in dozens of different phases. Some halls were all stone and flickering torches—others were gleaming wood wainscoting and silk wallpaper with chandeliers.

None of it looked like Death Valley Junction, which was kinda nice.

"We're almost there," Ana said. "It's in the oldest part."

Even though we were technically allowed to visit the library and move through the halls at night, it still felt like we were creeping through. The old stone walls, dark winding corridors, and flickering oil lamps made everything feel a bit surreal.

Ana stopped at two huge wooden doors. "Wait till you see this."

She pushed them open, revealing a massive space within. I stepped inside, awe flowing through me.

"Wow." I spun in a circle, absorbing it all.

The space was three stories high, and huge. Gleaming wooden shelves covered the walls, stuffed full of leather books with colorful spines. Ornate oil paintings hung on the walls—some even covering the books—and four large fireplaces burst to life as we entered. The ceiling overhead was shining, domed wood, and the furniture within was comfy and plush.

"This is amazing," I murmured. I sniffed deeply, taking in the scent of paper and ink.

"The fires aren't real," Ana said. "Just magic. But it makes it so cozy."

"Why is Potts such a grump if he gets to hang out here all day?"

"No idea." Ana wandered the space, eyeing the shelves and the long ladders that reached toward the ceiling.

I could live here—and I'd never really been much of a reader, even though I'd liked the idea. There just hadn't been money or time for books. I ran my fingertips over the smooth spine of one of the books, smiling.

"What are we looking for, exactly?" Ana asked. "Any clues?"

"Yeah. More clues." I'd been holding it in, both wanting to tell her and not wanting to speak of the craziness. Speaking of it would make it real. "When I was at—"

"Ooooooooh, oooooooooh."

I stopped dead, the ghostly moaning making my hair stand on end. I turned to Ana, who was frozen halfway up a ladder, her face white.

"Did you hear that?" I whispered.

"Yeah."

I looked around. The Pugs of Destruction were gone.

"Quit it, Chaos, Mayhem, and Ruckus," I said.

"Ooooooooh, oooooooooh."

"I don't think it's them." Ana slowly climbed down the ladder.

Shivering, I walked slowly around the massive room. "Hello?"

CHAPTER ELEVEN

"Ooooooooh, oooooooh."

The ghostly noise echoed through the cavernous library.

I shivered, at once nervous and delighted. It was a weird feeling.

"Are you a ghost?" I asked.

"Well, what else do you think makes that kind of noise?" A transparent young man drifted out from the shelves. Thick glasses made his eyes look large, and his clothes were some kind of older style. Eighteenth or nineteenth century, if I had to guess.

"Um, hi." How did one greet a ghost? Shake hands? "I'm Bree Blackwood."

"I'm Florian Bumbledomber, the librarian here."

"I thought that was Potts?"

Florian waved a hand. "Oh, that old hack. No, *I'm* the real librarian."

"I'm Ana." She waved.

"Good to meet you, Ana. Welcome to the night library." He spread his arms out, looking more like he should be on a stage than in a library. "I'm the night librarian. The *true* librarian."

"Nice to meet you. But why where you making the ghostly noises?" I asked.

"Entertainment, my dear." He bowed low. "Not many people come to visit in the evening. But you're a hard one to scare."

The disappointed look in his eyes clued me in. If I wanted info, I wanted this guy on my side. Especially since Potts was no fan of mine.

"Oh, no. I was terrified." I pointed to my face. "See how pale I am?"

He squinted, inspecting me. "I suppose it will do." He clapped his hands together. "So, what are you here for?"

"I want to know more about Njord, Rán, and Eir."

His brows rose. "Ahhh, interesting."

"You can help us?"

"To an extent. But you'll also have to help yourself." He gestured. "Come, come. You won't find your answers in this section."

I shared a glance with Ana, who shrugged. We followed him toward the far wall.

Which wasn't a true wall at all. He went to the left, where there was a large, wooden door hidden in a nook.

"Hardly anyone comes back here anymore." He pushed the door open.

A waft of cold air blew out, bringing with it the scent of leather and paper and magic. Tiny golden sparkles floated on the air.

I followed Florian through the door.

Awe spread through me, fierce and strong.

This was a library. It made the massive space we'd just come from look puny.

Florian swept out his arms, indicating the cavernous space filled with millions of books. It soared stories above us and dropped down stories below. We were somewhere in the middle of ten separate levels that surrounded a giant open space in the middle. It was much grayer and darker than the other library—but it was *huge.*

Light shined down from above, almost like streams of sunlight. But it was nighttime, so that had to be magic. Dust motes glittered in the air. Shining golden balls of light—or something—floated near the ceiling high above.

There were hundreds of nooks and crannies and different sections. It was a maze my mind could hardly comprehend.

"Welcome to my domain," Florian said. "The ghost library."

"Are they real books?" Ana asked.

They did lack a lot of the color the other library's books possessed.

"*Of course* they're real books." Florian scoffed. "I just call it that because it's my domain, and it sounds quite impressive, doesn't it?"

I nodded, not having to fake my enthusiasm. "It really does."

"And most of these books are quite old, hence their color," Florian said.

Ana walked toward the railing that protected us from falling into the pit in the center of the library. I looked for stairs, but found none. Here, we were blocked from the books.

"How do we get down?" I asked. "Or up."

"Good things don't come free, dearie."

"What do you mean?"

"You must contribute to the library if you want to gain from its knowledge. That is one way that we have obtained so many volumes."

My stomach dropped. I glanced at Ana, whose brow was creased with worry.

"What if we don't have anything to contribute?" I asked.

"It hardly seems fair," Ana said.

"Life isn't fair," Florian said.

He had that right.

"But you're in luck—*everyone* has something to contribute. Just think."

"That's all?" Ana asked.

"Not quite. But you'll have to figure the rest out for yourself." Florian backed up and sat in a wooden chair that was pressed against the wall, crossing his legs and folding his arms over his chest.

All right, then.

Ana and I looked around the platform, which was quite large. On the far end sat a table with a few chairs. Books were stacked on top, along with feather quills.

Ana and I approached.

"What do we have to contribute?" she whispered.

"I don't know." I frowned, searching my mind. "All we've ever done is fight monsters in Death Valley."

"Ooooh," Florian murmured.

I turned to him. "Is that a ghost noise or interest on your part?"

He frowned. "I've already scared you enough for one night."

I grinned, then looked at Ana. "I guess we were the only ones to successfully cross Death Valley multiple times."

"So, we'll give away our secrets?"

She had a point. Our monopoly on that information had set us up nicely to be the only ones transporting outlaws across the valley. It allowed us to command top dollar and keep up the payments on our concealment charms.

"We don't need that job anymore."

"Doesn't mean I don't want a backup," Ana said.

She had a point, and I couldn't blame her. Except I only felt a tiny sense of worry. It tugged at me, but the Protectorate tugged at me harder.

Ana, however, had always been more of a worrier than me. She was a Plan B and C kinda girl.

"It's like us symbolically cutting our ties with our old lives and committing to this place," she said.

"I know."

She sucked in a ragged breath, looking around. "You're right. Our old life was crap. It had moments of fun. But *this*. This is better." She squeezed my hand. "And we really need to figure out what the heck is happening with your magic."

I smiled and hugged her. "Thanks."

We sat down in the little wooden chairs. I grabbed a book and pulled it closer, flipping open the cover to reveal empty pages. "It'll take weeks to fill this. We don't have that kind of time."

"Let's just start. Maybe that'll prove we mean it."

"Yeah." I reached for a pen. Magic sparked up my fingertips as I picked it up. "What'll we call it?"

"A Treatise on the Monsters of Death Valley." Ana grinned. "Sounds good, huh?"

"Very." I put pen to paper on the title page, and the words magically appeared. They stretched across the paper in a fancy calligraphy that I would *never* be capable of. "Whoa."

"Yeah." Ana picked up a pen. "I'm going next."

I passed over the book. She turned a page and pressed her pen to the paper. Words raced over the white surface, describing the different terrains that one would encounter in the valley and how best to survive them.

"How'd you do that?" I asked.

"I just thought of it," she said.

"Cool." I took the book back and imagined fighting the Salt Monster on the Bad Water. A half second later, there was a detailed explanation on how to take him out.

We finished in less than ten minutes, then jumped up. I felt like a kid who had finished a test before anyone else, even though I'd never taken a real test in my life. I was lucky I could read—and the only reason I could do that was because my mom had taught me.

Actually, this fabulous library made me feel kinda dumb.

But I had a chance to learn here. Fighting monsters would always be my fave, but this place opened up a whole new world for me.

"You coming?" Ana asked.

Startled, I snapped out of it. "Yeah."

I walked toward Florian, who had fallen asleep with his chin resting on his chest.

"Florian?" I asked.

He jumped up, nearly tipping over his chair, and looked at us with startled eyes.

I held out the book. "That was awesome."

He took it and flipped through a page. "Nicely done." He grinned and swept out an arm.

The railing at the front of the platform disappeared, and wide, sweeping stairs appeared in its place.

"The library is yours." He started toward the stairs. "Now, follow me."

He led us down the stairs and onto the next level, then back behind some shelves and down some other stairs. As he directed us toward the far side, I peeked over the railing to see that the bottom of the library was a huge mosaic map.

Florian grabbed some huge books and set them on a wide wooden table. "You'll find what you need in there."

Barking sounded.

Florian sighed. "I must go. There are patrons who require a bedtime story."

He hurried off, and I turned toward Ana. "*That's* why the Pugs of Destruction respect the library?"

"They do like their stories. And they're quite intellectual."

All right, then.

I sat next to her and studied the largest book.

An Ancient Oral History of the Gods of the Norse.

"The Gods of the Norse? What do the Vikings have to do with

me?" I flipped open the pages and found the name Njord, skimming the surrounding text. "God of the sea?"

"And it says in this one that Rán is another sea goddess. She married Ægir, and they had nine daughters, known as the Daughters of Ægir."

"She really should get more credit for that. Daughters of Rán is really more fair."

"Agreed."

"But two gods of the sea—that explains my new water power. I'm not a god, though." Quickly, I flipped through, searching for the name Eir. I found it near the back. "Healing goddess of the Norse."

And I'd just healed Cade, saving him from a poison that had no antidote.

"Why am I developing powers associated with Norse gods?"

Ana shook her head, eyes wide. "I have no idea. But it's damned cool."

"And scary. I've lost my sonic boom power. Right after I gained the power of healing."

"*Lost?*" Her jaw dropped. She snapped it closed. "That's not possible."

"Apparently it is."

She shut her book. "Our next step needs to be talking to Arach."

"How, though? We went to the round room today in the hopes that she would come join us. If a problem as big as the dark curse wouldn't bring her, why would this?"

"I don't know, your godliness. But I think it's our best bet."

I punched her lightly in the arm. But she had a point. "Let's try to get some sleep for now. When the curse is fixed, we'll find a way to contact Arach. I want to know what the hell is going on with me."

And what could I expect from the future?

◇

Ana and I didn't see Florian or the Pugs of Destruction as we left the quiet library. It was nearly midnight, but that was the pugs' prime witching hour.

"I'm going to head to the armory real quick, okay?" I said.

"For what?"

"I want to see if they have a charm that can help me with my sonic boom power." I *hated* that it was gone, and the armorer, Coriandar, had once given me a charm to help control the sonic boom. Maybe he had one that could re-find it inside myself.

It was a total long shot, but I was desperate to try.

Ana squeezed my hand, understanding on her face. "Of course. Good luck."

"Thanks. See you bright and early."

She shot me a thumbs-up, then headed down the hall. I went in the opposite direction, getting lost only twice on my way to the armory. I'd realized last week that if you ever did get lost, you could say aloud the place you were headed to and the castle walls glowed, leading you on the right path.

It made you look like a real newb, though, so I didn't like to use it often.

The halls were quiet as I turned and went through the door leading to the underground armory. I hurried down the darkened stairwell, realizing too late that someone else was coming up.

I slammed into the tall, broad body. He grabbed me by the arms to steady me.

The scent of a storm at sea hit me.

"Cade." I looked up, catching sight of his handsome face cast in shadow.

He towered over me, boxing me into the wall in an attempt to keep me from falling on my butt. He was so close I could feel the heat of him radiating against my front, a delicious contrast to the cold stone wall at my back.

In the darkened stairwell, we were in a world of our own, trapped in a tiny bubble.

He let go of my arms, but instead of dropping his hands, he pressed them to the wall on either side of my head.

Time slowed to a crawl, and tension crackled between us. His gaze traced over my face.

"What are you doing here?" he murmured.

"Going to the armory." My eyes dropped to the strong column of his neck. To the delta at the base of his throat. I swallowed hard, barely managing to keep my mind out of the gutter. "You?"

"The same." His voice was rough, low.

He wasn't thinking about the armory. My gaze returned to his face. He looked so damned good in the low light, shadows cutting across his face and giving him a deliciously sinister air. It was an insanely hot contrast to how good I knew him to be.

All the desire and strain of the last two days pressed down on me. Desire glinted in his eyes as they dropped to my lips. His hands formed fists.

"I can't resist any longer." His voice was rough. Heavy.

Me neither. But the words didn't escape me. I moved the last few inches toward him—or he moved toward me. It was impossible to say.

But a moment later, my lips were crushed to his, and his strong arms wrapped around me, pulling me tight to his hard chest.

I could feel every hard curve of his muscles as I ran my hands up his chest and neck and sank my fingertips into his soft hair.

He groaned low against my lips, pressing me back against the wall until I could feel the full length of him against me. I shivered, pulling him as close as I could, and moved my lips against his.

His tongue slipped into my mouth, sending a streak of heat down my spine.

We stayed like that for minutes, hours, days, as he kissed the daylights out of me, making me nearly senseless with desire. I wanted to drag him back to my apartment and kick Mayhem off the bed. My head swam with pleasure.

But he pulled away, cheeks flushed and eyes hot. Through shortened breath, he gritted, "That's enough." He shook his head slowly. "It has to be enough."

"What?" Confusion clouded my mind.

"We can focus on the job now." Slowly, he released me, leaving me to lean against the wall. "We've gotten it out of our systems. I'll see you tomorrow morning."

He left me and strode up the stairs. Still gasping for breath, I watched him go.

Seriously?

I leaned against the wall. He might think we'd gotten that out of our systems, but he was *so* wrong.

~

The next morning, the whole team met in the entry hall. Cade looked at me as if nothing had happened last night.

Robot.

Last night, my visit to Coriandar might have been a bust since he couldn't help me, but that kiss with Cade hadn't been *nothing*.

"Ready?" Jude asked.

She stood next to Hedy and Ammons, along with two Demon Trackers who'd been introduced as Jack and Aria. They'd be in charge of setting up the massive magical bomb that would take out the portal. Emily was there for transport duty.

Ana, Cade, Caro, Ali, Haris, and I would go through to hunt whatever had sent this dark magic our way.

"We're all accounted for," Hedy said. "Let's go."

We headed out of the castle and onto the lawn. The bomb team went straight for the forest, while the rest of us walked toward the stables to get the buggy.

In our spare time between classes these last two weeks, we'd fixed it up and it looked good as new. In fairness, Ana had really led that charge since I'd been trying to get control of my magic.

We entered the horseless stables, and Ana leapt into the driver's seat and cranked the ignition.

"I'll take front platform." I climbed up onto it. "Avoid the spikes on the sides, guys. There might still be some Ravener poison on them."

"Aye aye." Caro saluted and climbed onto the back platform.

Haris joined her, while Ali leapt in next to Ana.

Cade joined me in the front, close enough on the small platform that I couldn't help but think of last night. Hell, he could be joining me in a football stadium and I'd still think of last night.

We said nothing, however, as Ana pulled the truck out of the stable and drove us across the lawn toward the forest.

By the time we arrived, the others were waiting for us.

"Potions." Jude handed out the little glass vials from Melusine. "You don't want this curse sticking to you."

Everyone downed theirs quickly, grimacing at the taste, then shoved the vials in their pockets.

Jude nodded. "All right. We'll go through in groups. The portal should be just wide enough for the truck. Once we're there, we'll transport to the city that contains the second portal. Cade and Bree will lead that, since they've been there before."

We all nodded. Though everyone could technically pile into the buggy, it would be too many people for even a powerful transport mage like Emily.

As planned, Ana drove the buggy through first. The Fae realm looked just as we'd left it, with the wide ocean on the right and the trees on the left. The beach stretched out for miles. I was damned grateful we wouldn't have to make that trek again since we now knew where we were headed.

Fortunately, there were no more oily monsters waiting for us.

The rest of our crew arrived a moment later.

Cade hopped off the truck and dug into his pocket for a transport stone. He met my gaze. "I'll see you there."

He was going to take the walkers, while the rest of us stayed in the buggy. I nodded.

Emily climbed up into the truck, joining me on the front platform. "Ready, guys?"

"Ready," Ana said.

I reached for Emily's hand.

"Envision where we're going," she said. "As clearly as you can."

I pictured the creepy decayed city and the enormous trees filled with VDBs. "Okay, go."

Emily's magic swirled on the air, and the ether sucked us in, throwing us across space through the Fae realm.

When I opened my eyes, we were in the middle of the abandoned Fae city, right next to the portal. The blackened trees towered overhead, and the buildings looked even more ramshackle and decayed. The stench of the portal's magic was so strong that I gagged.

A moment later, Cade appeared with the rest of the crew. They looked around, grimaces twisting their faces.

"This place is awful," Hedy said.

Jude looked straight at me. "You have four hours. See if you can stop the curse and learn what you can. But after four hours, we close this portal for good."

I nodded, determined to do the job right.

Cade loped over to the buggy and leapt onto the top next to me. It was a tight fit.

Ana ducked down to grab something off the floor and handed a tangle of climbing harnesses to Ali. "Hand those out." She looked at me and grinned. "Safety first!"

I nodded, taking my harness and clipping it onto the rail. It was quick release, so if I had to get out, I could. But sometimes the driving got hairy in these situations.

I pointed to the portal well, which was surrounded by the

same low, stone wall. The buggy's tires should be able to handle it. "Just drive right in. I'll take care of the rest." I looked at the group. "And everyone—hold your breath."

Ana saluted, then revved the engine and drove the buggy straight into the well. The big tires climbed up and over the little stone wall, then the heavy front of the car plunged down into the darkness.

CHAPTER TWELVE

This time, I didn't give the water a chance to submerge us.

I reached for it with my magic, pressing it backward, forcing the masses of liquid away from the buggy. My stomach jumped into my throat as we fell through the blackness, wind whipping my hair back from my face.

Then the ether sucked us in, taking control.

When it spat us out in the hellscape on the other side, the buggy was upright, sitting on its wheels.

"Holy fates!" Ana cried. "That was amazing."

"And *this* is terrifying," Ali said.

I had to agree.

This realm was just as dark and scary as it had been. Lightning cracked in the sky, revealing a long expanse of land prowled by oil monsters, rows of giant, thorny black hedges, and the massive beasts near the building on the hill.

The stench of the curse made my eyes water and my stomach lurch.

As if on cue, the oil monsters that roamed the land in front of us turned to face us, their gaping black mouths revealing white fangs.

"They look like the aliens from that movie," Ali said.

"*Alien?*" Ana asked.

"That's the one." Ali grinned. "Now let's fight these bastards."

"Couldn't have said it better myself." Ana lay on the gas and laughed. The buggy shot toward the monsters, who'd started to run toward us.

There were at least two dozen. I drew my sword and shield. There was no water in sight, and my sonic boom power was officially kaput, so it had to be hand-to-hand.

Next to me, Cade drew his shield from the ether and hurled it toward a group of oncoming monsters. The silver disk flew through the air, beheading three of the beasts one after the other. Black oil spurted into the air from the stumps of their necks.

From behind, I heard Caro laughing. I glanced back. She was shooting her water jets at the creatures, turning them into oily, black puddles.

These things were *weird*.

And then it was my turn. One of them had neared the truck and leapt for me, long arms outstretched and claws glinting in the glow of the lightning. The impressions where its eyes should've been were fixed right on me as it grabbed onto the truck railing.

I slammed my shield down, knocking away the arm, and then sliced out with my blade, leaving a deep gouge in the chest of the creature. It fell back, splatting onto the ground.

Ali and Haris fought with swords, seeming unwilling to try their possession trick with the oily creatures.

"Why don't you possess them?" Ana called.

"They're made of magic, not flesh and blood." Ali hacked at a beast with his blade.

I kept busy on the front of the buggy, along with Cade, using my sword to hack away at the monsters that jumped up to grab the front railing. They left black streaks where their hands gripped and stunk like fetid garbage.

Ana just plowed right through them, giving us a relatively stable platform from which to work. The only downside was the splatter, and soon my clothes were flecked with evil, black oil.

When one of the creatures nearly managed to make it over the railing, I kicked out, nailing him in the chest. He flew backward, but not before one long claw reached out and sliced at my calf.

Pain welled.

I winced, then turned to face the next monster, trying to ignore the ache, and stabbed him in the throat. He clawed at the blade, and I used my shield to shove him onto the ground.

All around us, the oily bodies soaked into the dirt.

"Incoming!" Cade shouted.

Ahead of us, six of the monsters had formed a pyramid, holding each other aloft high into the air. They wanted Ana to plow through them so they could toss one *into* the buggy.

Holy crap, these bastards were smart. Who created them?

"I'm gonna swerve!" Ana said.

"No, take them out!" I cried. "We've got this."

"All right!" She rummaged around on the seat next to her, then tossed me a pair of the sand goggles I normally wore in the desert.

I caught them. "Thanks!"

She tossed another pair, and Cade caught them. He pulled them on.

"Here we go!" Ana laid on the gas, and the buggy jumped forward.

I looked at Cade. "You go high. I'll go low."

He nodded, his handsome face concealed by the goggles and streaked with the creepy, black oil. He looked like some kind of steampunk oil rig worker.

I raised my blade and crouched slightly. I'd need my balance for this.

Ana plowed into the pyramid of monsters, immediately

pulverizing three of them. Their oil splashed and exploded, coating me. I could still see through the goggles, but there were dozens of little flecks of black on them.

The other three oil monsters leapt for us, flying through the air with their claws outstretched.

I raised my shield. One of the beasts slammed into it, sending vibrations up my arm. It reached out, raking claws down my bicep.

I lowered the shield and stabbed the beast in the shoulder, tearing my blade to the left. The creature whirled from the force, and I kicked it in the gut, sending it over the platform.

Cade had just beheaded one, which was now a puddle on the platform, and was sending his sword through the middle of another. I lent a helping sword, slicing through the creature's neck.

It collapsed in a puddle of oil.

"Gross." I was covered in the stuff.

"Well done!" Ana cried.

"That's the last of them!" Caro called.

I looked around, realizing we'd taken out every single one. They were puddles of oil dotted over the dark landscape, gleaming in the light of the constantly striking lightning.

Cade caught my eye. "Good job."

I pulled off the goggles, grateful to see again. "Yeah. Not a bad team."

He grinned, pulling off his goggles. The skin around his eyes was pretty much the only clean part of him. He lifted a shirt to wipe at the oil, revealing a swatch of hard stomach and smooth skin.

I turned away, ignoring the *extremely* poorly timed warmth in my belly—and inspected the oncoming barrier of thorny hedges. Lightning strikes illuminated them, revealing them to be all thorns and branches—not a single leaf. The thorns were each about a foot long. Wooden daggers.

"Twenty bucks those thorny things start whipping out at us!" Haris called.

"Not taking that bet," Ali said.

"Me neither," Caro said. "You always take the obvious ones."

I eyed them, considering. There were at least four rows of deadly hedges between us and the giant monsters prowling the yard in front of the big brick building. There were gaps in the hedges that we could drive through, but they were all narrow.

The thorny limbs could strike out at us. There were so many that we probably couldn't beat them all off. And what if they hit a tire?

I glanced back at Ana, who grinned at me.

"Thinking what I'm thinking?" she said.

"Yep. But don't slow the car."

"As if I would *ever*." She shot me a mock offended look.

I stashed my sword and shield in the ether, and my body fell into the remembered routine of switching places while on the road. Ana and I were used to this kind of shit—we might be newbs at the Academy, but this kind of thing was our jam.

I unhooked my harness and moved toward the cockpit.

"Put your foot on the gas, Ali," Ana said.

We used to pull this maneuver with Rowan, but after she'd disappeared, we'd usually get a client to help us make the switch.

Ali did as instructed, sticking his leg down into the well and pressing on the gas. Ana unhooked her seatbelt and climbed over the railing onto the front platform. She kept a hand on the wheel until I grabbed it as I climbed into the driver's seat and took her place.

I pressed my foot to the gas. "I got it."

Ali let go.

The car never slowed.

"Everyone get low!" Ana said. She looked back at me. "Punch it."

I laid on the gas and the buggy leapt forward. Everyone

crouched low except for Ana, who raised her hands. Her magic swelled on the air, and her shimmery pearlescent shield formed around us. It covered the buggy like a dome.

As we neared the first row of thorny hedges, I felt a sharp prickling against my skin. A warning. *There's more where this came from.*

The first branch lashed out at Ana, cracking against her shield and shattering into shards of wood. The shield flared white from the impact, but held strong. Another thorny vine flew, this one larger. It smashed against Ana's shield. She winced, crouching low, but kept her shield strong.

My stomach jumped as a massive branch slammed into my sister's shield. Sweat rolled down her temples from the strain.

I pressed harder on the gas, giving the buggy every bit of speed it could manage. The massive tires ate up the ground, bumping over rocks and dirt.

"Almost there!" I yelled.

Ana's shield was almost opaquely white from all the blows it'd received. She was sweating and red-faced, her muscles trembling.

By the time we made it to the other side, everyone looked tense. Ana dropped her shield immediately, sagging against the railing. Cade grabbed her, keeping her from falling into the gross oily puddle on the platform.

"I got it. I'm good." Ana panted and stood.

I slowed the vehicle a bit, dropping down from the mad 100 mph we'd been doing to a more reasonable 60. This wasn't exactly highway-grade land, and the only light we had came from the lightning strikes.

"Let's trade," Ana said.

I nodded.

Ana had just started to climb over the railing when Caro screamed. "Watch out!"

My gaze darted up, away from Ana and toward the ground ahead of us.

It'd risen up like a wave of dirt. A *wall* of dirt.

Oh shit.

Caro hurtled past me, having leapt off the back platform like a gazelle, and climbed onto the front platform next to Cade. Ana tumbled off into the front seat.

Caro threw out her hands, directing a sharp stream of water toward the earthen wave.

The magical water hose cut through the dirt from left to right, slicing it down the middle. The stuff collapsed, the wall of dirt crumbling down.

"Hang on!" I swerved right, barely managing to avoid the massive pile of earth that would wreak havoc on the front of the buggy. The left tires rode up on the edge of the dirt pile, nearly tipping us.

Cade and Caro clung to the railings at the front. My seatbelt cut hard into my skin, and Ali kept an exhausted Ana from tumbling out the side of the car. Haris whooped, clearly enjoying our near crash.

The buggy slammed upright back onto the ground. I let up on the gas just a bit.

"We're almost to the giant monsters!" I looked at Ana, the question in my eyes.

"Yeah, I'll drive." She straightened, already looking a bit better. She'd used up a lot of magic back there—most of it, if I had to guess—but there was no room for quitting.

We made the trade as Caro returned to her spot in the back, and I climbed up next to Cade.

Ahead of us, four giant beasts prowled. From a distance, it'd been hard to determine *what* exactly they were.

Up close, it wasn't any easier.

"They look like a cross between boars and alligators," Ali said.

"HellBeast," Cade said. "Straight from Hell. Kill one, and it'll wake up back home, sleeping at the foot of Satan."

"Good," Haris said. "We'll take care of two of them. Send them back to Daddy."

Ana drove toward the monsters, the last obstacle between us and the big building that gleamed black under every lightning strike. The HellBeasts turned toward us, eyes blazing red and bright.

We were about twenty yards from them when Ali shouted, "We're out!"

"See you later!" Haris jumped off the back of the truck. Ali followed. They sprinted away from the buggy.

"Hey, Uggo!" Ali shouted.

One of the beasts turned and raced after him, massive feet pounding at the earth.

Haris ran straight at the HellBeast closest to him. The creature's eyes were riveted to the buggy, but Haris raised a hand to his mouth and whistled. The sound pierced the night, loud and sharp.

The creature's head swung left, its eyes gleaming. Then it charged for Haris.

Haris charged it right back, leaping up just as the beast neared him and disappearing into its face.

Weird.

The creatures stopped, stood stock-still, then jerked toward one of its fellows, looking like a beast yanking against a lead.

Haris was clearly trying to get it to attack one of the other monsters, but it was resisting. Unwilling to fight its brethren?

Ali's creature was doing the same. They appeared to give up at the same time. Both possessed monsters sprinted for the brambles, away from us.

"Woo! Nice!" Ana called.

I grinned. This was monster fighting of the best variety. We'd send them right back to Hell, where they probably preferred being anyway.

Cade pointed his sword toward the monster on the left. "I'll take him."

"Have fun."

He grinned. "See you later."

He stashed his sword and shield in the ether, then leapt off the buggy, easily catching his footing on the ground, and sprinted toward one of the monsters. He shifted as he ran, blue light swirling around him to reveal the massive wolf. He might be four times bigger than a normal wolf, but the demon monster dwarfed him.

Cade leapt for the beast's throat.

Caro appeared next to me on the front platform. "Let's tag team this last one."

"Deal."

The beast was about thirty feet away, prowling toward us. Ana slowed the buggy. Caro raised her hands and shot a jet of water at it. It plowed into the beast's shoulder, blasting straight through it.

The creature roared.

"I'm a bit tapped out." Caro panted. "Won't be able to do much of this."

She shot it again, in the leg this time. It roared, thrashing its alligator-shaped head. I leapt off the buggy, stumbling briefly, then charged the creature.

The rank scent of its magic was indistinguishable from the horrible curse stink that flowed from the huge building. It was bad enough to make my eyes water.

Caro hit the creature one last time, straight in the chest. The beast slowed, going to a knee. I ran, leaping onto its leg and then scrambling onto its back. Its leathery hide scratched my hands like sandpaper.

Something pale blue in its mouth caught my eyes. A tiny baby sock?

This thing ate *babies*?

Oh, this thing had to go.

The creature shook like a dog, trying to throw me off, but I clung to its neck. It paused long enough to allow me to rise up and call my sword from the ether.

The hilt appeared in my hand. I punched the blade down into the creature's skull. I grunted at the impact, driving the blade deep.

The beast shuddered and fell, immediately disappearing in a poof of dusty, dark magic. Returning to Hell.

I crashed against the ground, covered in the dusty remains of HellBeast.

"Gross." I spat out black dust, which stuck to every inch of my skin that was covered in the black oil. "This place is seriously disgusting."

Across the way, Cade polished off the last HellBeast, tearing out its throat in a spray of black blood. Ana and Caro had made a big loop to pick up Ali and Haris, who'd lost their beasts somehow. I wasn't sure I wanted to know what they'd done to them, to be honest.

The buggy sped toward me. I staggered to my feet.

Whatever was inside that creepy, black building had better be impressive, considering the protections that surrounded it.

The crew on the buggy clapped as they approached.

"Well done!" Ali shouted.

Caro grinned and reached down off the front platform, offering to give me a hand up as Ana slowed the buggy. I grabbed her hand and jumped, scrambling over the railing.

Cade loped back to us, his gray wolf muzzle streaked with black HellBeast blood. He leapt into the air, shifting in a flash of blue light before landing on the platform next to us.

"Not bad." Caro nodded. "You trainees know your shit."

I bowed. "Thank you, thank you."

But the moment of levity was brief.

Ana was driving us closer to the creepy building, and it was hard not to notice the strength of the dark magic surrounding it. I'd almost become inured to the stink, but it managed to surprise me.

Worse, my muscles felt weaker. My brain a bit foggier.

"Do you guys feel that?" Ana asked.

"Aye," Cade said. "The curse definitely originates from here."

The exterior walls and the building were entirely black from it, the walls looking crumbled and decayed. There was one exterior wall that surrounded the property lawn. Through the wrought iron gate, I caught sight of a large building within.

"I think you can ram it," I said. The buggy, with its reinforced grille meant specifically to break through things, was perfect for the job.

"Everyone get off the front platform," Ana said.

We climbed off, finding seats in the main cockpit. Ali and Haris took the back seat.

"Hang on!" Ana pressed on the gas, and the buggy jumped forward. She laughed as she sped toward the gate at breakneck speed.

The vehicle plowed through, breaking apart the iron gate in an explosion of metal. Dark magic surrounded our vehicle.

CHAPTER THIRTEEN

I gagged at the increased strength of the dark magic and looked around. The interior of the compound reminded me a bit of the castle, with a large lawn and the scent of the sea. Skeletal oak trees reached for the dark sky, their tips blackened by lightning. In the middle sat a large, square building. It looked old, but details were obscured by the black, sooty curse that covered every inch of it.

A broken fountain sat in the middle of it all, a relic of a time when this place was maintained.

There was no one around, and the abandoned air was strong.

"There's no way this place is actually empty," I said. "There has to be guards or—"

As if on cue, figures spilled out of the large doors in the middle of the building. They were each cloaked in black, with hoods covering their faces. Some had horns sticking out from the cloaks.

The demons roared and charged us, weapons glinting in the light. One hurled a fireball that Ana dodged around. It plowed into the ground near us.

"Out of the buggy!" Ana said.

She was right. No need to draw their fire here. We didn't want to lose our ride out. We couldn't walk back in the time we had before the portal closed. I figured we were down to about two hours now.

She stopped the vehicle, and we piled out, racing for the demons.

Next to me, my friends plunged into battle. Ali and Haris possessed any demon that got near them. The demons immediately began to fight each other, with Ali and Haris jumping out of their bodies before the death blow took its effect.

Caro drew a sword and lunged for the demon nearest her. Her water power was probably running low, but she could do some serious damage with that blade.

Ana hurled her daggers, while Cade drew his sword.

I eyed the fountain, feeling the water within. I called to it, picking it up like I had an invisible bucket, and slamming it into the demon who charged me.

It plowed into him, sending him flying onto his face with enough force that he left a foot-deep skid mark in the dirt.

He didn't get up.

Damn, I could move some water.

I could feel even more of it, coming from behind this building. The ocean? A lake? It was a little bit too far away for me to use, but knowing it was there was cool.

I fought my way toward the great wooden doors, using my sword to take out any demon that stood in my way. They were fast, however. One slammed a fireball into my shin, leaving a shining red burn that sang with pain at every step.

But I was closer. Only twenty feet from the door now, and a path was cleared.

"Go!" Caro shouted. "We'll take care of the rest."

Ana, Cade, and I were the ones closest to the door. There were still a dozen demons left.

"You sure you can handle this?" I shouted.

Haris and Ali just laughed.

Well, that settled that.

"Thanks!" I raced for the door, dodging a fire mage's blast.

I yanked open the wooden door, Cade and Ana at my side. We hurried into an empty entry foyer. A flickering, candle-filled chandelier hung from the ceiling, illuminating the gloomy interior.

The curse had blackened the entire space, including a large crucifix on the far wall.

"A monastery," Cade said.

"Not a monastery anymore." I looked around. "No way monks did this."

"No. It's been reused." Ana brushed away some of the blackness from the ground with her foot. "Look at this."

I peered down. A nine-sided star had been gouged into the floor. Burned into it.

That was new.

I touched the back of my neck where my own star-shaped mark was hidden. Mine was only four points. I shook my head. Had to be a coincidence.

But when Ana's worried gaze met mine, I wasn't so sure.

I looked away. "Come on. We need to hurry."

I started left, having no idea where to go now that we were here. Maybe we'd get lucky and meet a helper like Squido, though I doubted it.

As a group, we crept through the quiet hall of the building. Magic vibrated on the air, even stronger than it had been out on the lawn.

"Feel that?" I asked.

"Aye," Cade murmured.

"Coming from a person, I think," Ana said.

She was right. I couldn't get an exact handle on the magical signature—the reek of the curse was too great for that—but it had a distinct living feel to it. Magical signatures from objects usually felt a bit more dead without the strong sensory output living magical signatures had.

The hall we crept through was abandoned, every inch covered in the dark curse. Flicking oil lamps lit our way. Would there be more guards here?

We passed doors to empty rooms, but none caught my eye until we saw one where a relatively clean desk sat.

"Guys," I whispered and pointed to the desk. "Check that out."

"It's not hit by the curse," Ana murmured.

I went toward the room, making sure it was empty before I snuck in.

"Guard the door," I said to Cade.

He nodded and set up guard.

Maybe I should feel a little bad about bossing him around, but he was the best option for brute force defense.

And I was close to answers. I could feel it.

There was nothing I wanted more than answers. Why had one of those oily monsters called my name? Called me here?

My heart thundered as I crept through the room, waiting for someone to jump out at me even though I'd seen no one here.

The only two pieces of furniture were a single desk and chair. Though there was nothing on the desk, I rooted through the drawers. Blank paper, pens, nothing of importance.

My fingertips brushed the leather cover of a book. A tiny book. I pulled it out.

A nine-pointed star was drawn on the front. I glanced up at Ana, whose eyes were bright with excitement.

"That's gotta be a clue," she said.

I flipped it open, catching sight of the words *Dei Rebelles*.

Dei? Wasn't that Latin for gods?

There was no time to read it, so I stuck it in the inner pocket of my jacket then scanned the room. There was another open door. I headed toward it.

Within, there was just a simple, narrow bed—perfect for an

ancient monk—and a chair. A pair of black leather high heels sat on the floor, right under a black cloak hanging from a peg on the wall.

"A woman," Ana murmured.

"The same one Ricketts mentioned before he died?" Or was it just a giant coincidence?

I never liked coincidences.

I backed out of the room. "Let's go find her."

"Ready?" Cade asked from where he stood at the door, sword drawn and stance ready.

"Yeah." We slipped out into the quiet hall again, moving deeper into the house. Magic prickled more insistently against my skin. "I think we're getting close."

The next room we entered was massive, like an old ballroom. Or chapel, maybe. It was too dark to say, with only one little chandelier lighting the whole place. Had the person who'd spread this curse killed all the monks, or had they left long ago?

Movement by the far wall caught my eye.

Two huge figures stepped forward. My head tilted back to take in their insane size. Each was draped in a leather kilt, their massive hands gripping huge wooden clubs. Squashed faces completed the look.

"Ogres," Ana said.

"Holy fates." I'd never seen real ogres before, but I'd heard of them. They were huge—thirty feet tall, at least.

And they were guarding another door.

"Whatever we want, it's behind those doors." I pointed to them.

"I'll take care of the ogres. You two go in," Cade said.

From a safety standpoint, it was smarter to stick together. But I really didn't want to lose whatever was on the other side. If we'd cut through the last of their guards, they might run for it.

And Cade was really damned capable, no matter how much I might pointlessly worry.

"Perfect, thanks," I said.

"Just give me one moment." He raised his shield, drew back, and then hurled it at the ogre on the left.

The disk flew through the air, too fast for the ogre to process. It slammed into his skull, throwing him onto his back. The shield returned to Cade, snapping onto his arm.

He threw it again, but the second ogre knew what to expect. It ducked at the last moment.

"Maybe he's the smart one," Ana said.

Cade caught the returning shield and grinned. "Let's go. I'll keep him off your back."

We sprinted for the door, Cade veering off to fight the ogre.

Ana and I slipped through the door, straight out into the dark night.

I gaped at the sight.

We were outside, the lightning striking high overhead. The sound of waves crashing sounded from below. This was a cliff overlooking the sea.

In front of us, a glass orb contained a tall woman who was liberally coated in the same shiny, black oil that had covered the monsters we'd first fought. Her head was tilted back and her hands raised high, palms open.

"Is she trapped?" Ana asked.

I studied the ground around her glass globe enclosure. It was streaked with the black oil, which tapered out to form the same black stain that coated the building and stretched into the Fae realm. And finally into the Protectorate.

Evil surrounded her.

No. Evil was her.

This was all coming from her. The globe seemed to be taking the dark magic from her and feeding it into the ground.

I'd never seen anything like it. Never even heard of such a thing.

"I think she's the source of the curse," I murmured.

At that moment, the woman's head snapped forward.

Green eyes blazed, searing me. She grinned, her teeth a bright white contrast to the pitch-black oil that coated her body.

The globe exploded outward, thousands of glass shards streaking through the air. I ducked behind my shield, Ana lunging in next to me, but they sliced at my legs.

Pain seared. I winced.

When the glass stopped flying, I lowered the shield and peered over. The woman took a step toward us, her grin large.

Confusion and fear raced through me. Part of me screamed to hurl a dagger at her and finish her; the other part wanted answers. I couldn't use my water power. Dragging her out to sea wouldn't get me what I wanted.

I resisted my usual fight-or-fight response, and called out, "Why are you doing this?"

She laughed, a throaty sound that was deeper than a normal human voice. "I would think that is obvious."

"It's really not," Ana said.

The woman's gaze moved to me. I tried to take in every detail I could about her, but the sleek, black oil obscured her features and slicked back her hair. Even her body and the type of clothes she wore was hard to determine.

But her power wasn't. It stank of evil. Just like the curse.

"You are the curse," I said.

"Impressed?"

"No. But why the hell are you doing this?" Carefully, I stashed my sword in the ether and pulled out my dagger, making sure to do so behind the concealment of my shield.

If I had any choice in the matter, this wouldn't be a close-range attack. I didn't want to get anywhere *near* this woman.

"I would think that's obvious, *Bree*."

"How do you know me?"

Her head turned toward Ana. *"Ana."*

Ana growled low in her throat. Her magic vibrated around

her, weak and faint. She'd blown most of it getting us past the thorny hedges.

"Why this curse?" I asked. "Do you want to kill us?"

"It's not what I want that matters." She shook her head, the way someone did when they heard unwanted voices. Her gaze snapped to me. "The curse was the best way to get to you. Either it destroyed the protections on your castle, or it brought you to me." She grinned. "Fortunately, you couldn't bear to wait."

She was hunting me the same way Ricketts had been. This *was* the woman who'd helped him. The woman he'd worked for.

"What is *Dei Rebelles*?" I asked.

"Maybe you're not so stupid after all." She raised her hands, ready to use her magic. "And you'll find out soon enough."

"Get ready," I murmured to Ana.

I hurled my dagger as she threw a lightning bolt at us. We dived left, barely avoiding the strike.

My blade sliced her arm, and she hissed.

Ana threw one of her daggers, but the woman was too fast. She zapped it with a lightning bolt.

I dived left, trying to distract her.

It worked.

Too well. Her lightning bolt hit me in the leg, sending bone-numbing pain tearing through me. I stumbled, crashing to the ground. She threw another bolt at me. I huddled behind my shield, my arms shaking from the impact.

Ana threw another dagger. It plunged into the woman's other arm. She shrieked her rage, yanking the blade out and raising her arms.

All around, rocks began to roll toward her. Large ones and small ones dug themselves out of the earth. She flung her hands out toward us. The rocks veered off course, rolling toward Ana and me. Faster and faster. Some were as large as small cars.

They'd crush us.

My heart rate spiked. I couldn't fight this with sword or shield.

And Ana didn't have much shield magic left.

I called upon the ocean, praying I'd have the accuracy and skill I needed. I just had to buy time until our friends arrived and we could capture her. Get the answers I craved.

As if she could tell what I was doing, the woman threw out her arms and shot another lightning bolt at me. Thunder cracked on the air as it lit up the night sky.

Ana shrieked and charged, throwing out the last of her protective magic to create a shield in front of me. The lightning struck it, turning it white.

That brief moment was all I needed. My magic grabbed onto the ocean far below and dragged the water upward.

I envisioned a two-pronged wave. Strain pulled at my muscles and my magic. The sea was far away, difficult to grasp. I panted, giving it everything I had. Feeding my magic into the ocean as I commanded it to come to me.

Fear chilled me—this couldn't possibly work.

The wall of water appeared, rising tall above the cliff, and crashed down on the boulders that rolled toward us, narrowly avoiding the woman.

The rocks were so close to us that the crashing water soaked me and my sister.

I commanded the water to drag the rocks into the sea. It bubbled and thrashed, pulling the rocks away from us and over the cliff edge.

Wow. I couldn't believe that had worked. Water was powerful —but *that* powerful?

The woman shrieked her rage, raising her hands again.

Then her head jerked, her green gaze going wide as she spotted something behind us.

I glanced back, spotting Cade and our friends.

"Capture, don't kill!" I shouted.

The woman hissed, then turned and sprinted for the cliff.

"No!" I raced after her, dropping my shield and sword. My lungs burned as I ran.

She jumped, sailing through the air.

Disappearing.

I skidded to a stop at the edge of the cliff, watching her plunge toward the ocean. The splash far below was tiny, the streak of oil on top like a bloodstain.

I recoiled, feeling the revulsion of the ocean as she plunged into its depths. Gagging, I called upon my magic, begging the ocean to find her. To return her to me.

I wanted her so badly I could taste it on my tongue like blood after a bite. She had *answers*.

I lifted the water in waves and spires, but the woman never appeared.

Ana joined me, panting.

"It's not working." Frustration beat at my chest, strong and fierce.

"She's gone."

Cade, Caro, Ali, and Haris joined us. I could feel their presence but didn't turn to look. *I had to get her.* I pushed my magic harder, searching the sea for her. Perhaps I was going crazy, but I thought I could see beneath the ocean in my mind's eye.

Rocks and silver fish and kelp. But no woman.

My breath heaved and my muscles ached. Weakness replaced the magic within me.

"Stop!" Ana's voice came from far away.

I ignored her, still searching for the woman, moving the sea below. My head buzzed. My body sagged.

Strong arms wrapped around me, tugging at me. I thrashed.

"Stop!" Cade's voice was low in my ear. "Stop. She's gone."

Frustration welled within me, but I sagged, panting.

Damn it.

She was gone. And my magic was tapped out.

Cade kept me supported as I regained my footing. I took half a moment to rest against his broad chest and draw on his strength. Then I sucked in a deep breath and stood on my own, pulling away.

I turned to my friends. "Let's get out of here."

They nodded. Each looked like hell, covered in oil and black dust and blood and bruises.

"How long do we have?" Ana asked.

Caro looked at a slim watch on her wrist. "An hour. Let's hurry. The demons and monsters are all dead, but we don't want to hit any snags."

Wasn't that the truth. This was the last place I wanted to hang out.

We turned and ran back across the lawn. Inside the huge room, both of the ogres lay on their backs, out cold. I made a mental note to ask Cade how he'd taken out the second one.

As we ran through the empty building, I realized the black soot was fading from the walls.

"It's returning to normal," Ana said.

"Thank fates." It was more than I could have hoped for.

The trip back across the challenge field was fortunately uneventful. With the woman's curse no longer fueling this place, the thorny hedges had gone silent, returning to normal.

By the time Ana drove us through the portal, I was beyond ready to get home.

Jude and Hedy were the first ones we saw as we arrived back in Eidollawn. Their eyes brightened, and relief relaxed their faces.

"Thank fates you're back," Jude said.

"And you succeeded?" Hedy gestured to the buildings around us, which were beginning to lose some of their oily stain.

"Mostly," I said. "Stopped the curse, but not the one who cast it."

"We'll discuss that more later," Jude said. "For now, we'll shut this portal for good so that the curse can't hurt this place again."

"Back up," Hedy said. "Let's detonate this thing."

We retreated to the protection of one of the buildings. All around the portal, Hedy had laid orange crystals connected by golden wire. Magic vibrated around them.

"It's like magical C4," she murmured. "Designed to break a portal's magic. A little invention I made up."

"Nice," I murmured.

She raised her wand and muttered a few words, then flicked it toward the crystals. They exploded in a blast of fiery light. Then the portal and the well collapsed. The magic that had flowed from it disappeared entirely, leaving a blank space that I could almost feel. A lack of all magic—right there, in that one little spot.

"Well done." Jude brushed her hands together. "Now, let's get out of here."

I gave the well one last look. Longing, almost. For the woman who'd disappeared, and the answers she'd taken with her.

CHAPTER FOURTEEN

An hour later, I stumbled into my apartment, exhausted and utterly filthy. At least my wounds were healed, courtesy of my new power over healing. That was one badass magical gift.

My mind swam with all that I'd seen and learned, and it took me a moment to notice Mayhem on the couch.

She looked up, a giant turkey leg clutched in her jaws.

"Mixing it up?" I asked.

She woofed without dropping the meat.

Aching, I shrugged out of my jacket. My hand brushed against the little book that was still inside the interior pocket. I pulled it out, frowning as I studied it.

"I don't suppose you know what *Dei Rebelles* means?" I asked Mayhem.

She woofed again, but it sounded exactly the same as the first woof, and I didn't speak ghost pug, so I just smiled. "Yeah, me neither."

I set the book on the counter and snagged an energy drink out of the fridge on my way to the shower. We had a debriefing in an hour—after everyone washed the oil and stink off themselves—and I definitely needed a pick-me-up if I was going to make it that long.

In my bathroom, Ruckus sat in the sink, bubbles up to his neck. He barked happily at me, his little fangs glinting in the bathroom light.

"Just clean up after yourself," I muttered tiredly, unable to help the grin that spread across my face.

The shower revived me somewhat—along with the energy drink that I chugged while the soap was washing out of my hair—and by the time I got out, I was ready to face Jude and Hedy.

Had I succeeded at this test?

True, we'd stopped the curse. But technically, I'd also lost the woman who *was* the curse.

I wanted to find her for my own satisfaction—she had answers I desperately wanted.

But I also wanted to pass this damned test and advance up the ranks at the Academy. I liked working cases like this way more than I liked training. Training sucked. This was...fun. In a weird way.

Quickly, I dressed, then headed down into the living room. Mayhem waited for me, a small book clutched in her mouth.

"Mayhem!"

I knelt by her. She dropped the book on the floor.

Latin Dictionary.

I picked it up, glancing at her. "You *do* know what *De Rebelles* means?"

Was my ghost dog smarter than me?

She yipped.

Yeah, my ghost dog was smarter than me.

"Thanks." I tried to pet her head, but my hand just tingled where it touched her ghostly self.

She yipped again, then returned to the corner where she'd stashed her turkey leg. I laughed, kinda grossed out. Here I had this beautiful new apartment and a ghost pug stored her turkey leg in the corner.

Oh well. I'd take Mayhem over a clean apartment any day.

Aching, I climbed to my feet and picked up the little book off the counter. I tucked it into my jacket pocket and left the tower. In the main hall, I flipped through the dictionary as I walked. It took me a while—and some bumping into things—but I finally figured out what *Dei Rebelles* meant.

Rebel Gods.

Dang.

That didn't sound good.

Everyone was waiting for me in the debriefing room. I took a seat between Ana and Cade, my gaze on Hedy and Jude. Caro, Ali, and Haris sat next to them.

Ana handed me a PB&J sandwich. My heart jumped.

"I thought you'd be hungry, and I'd made one for myself," she said.

"I love you." I took the sandwich and chomped in. Man, I loved PB&J. Candy sandwiches.

"Well, what happened in there?" Jude asked.

I swallowed the bite of my sandwich, then explained the old monastery and the woman within. The memory of her dark magic made me shiver.

"We think she's the same woman who gave Ricketts the magic he needed to capture me," Ana said.

"And the same woman who gave him the *orders* to capture you," I said. "She was behind this all along."

Jude tapped her chin. "So, when your concealment charm failed two weeks ago and the intruder gained entrance to the castle, she learned where you were. But this time, she decided to break in from another direction."

"Exactly."

"We'll station guards by the Magic's Bend and Edinburgh portals," Jude said. "Until we catch her."

It was a good idea. The portals would only permit you entrance if you were a member of the Protectorate or escorted by one, but there was no telling what this woman was capable of.

"The question is, *why* does she want you so badly?" Hedy asked.

"I have no idea." But she had to be one of the ones who'd hunted us since we were children. It only made sense.

Finally, they'd caught up to us.

At least we had the Protectorate on our side now.

I pulled the book out of my pocket and put it on the table. "I did find this, though. The front page is in Latin. It says *Rebel Gods.*"

Next to me, Cade stiffened.

Hedy gasped, and Jude gripped the armrests of her chair.

"Rebel Gods?" Cade's voice was soft. Dangerous.

"Yeah." I looked between them, my heartbeat pounding in my ears. This was important. Very important.

"Why is everyone freaking out?" Ana asked.

Caro, Ali, and Haris looked as confused as I felt. But the people in charge looked like they'd seen a ghost.

"Tell me what it means," I said. "What are the Rebel Gods? Was *she* a Rebel God?"

"We wouldn't have won that battle if she had been," Cade said.

"We need to consult with the other department heads," Jude said. "And Arach."

"You know she doesn't come when called," Hedy said.

Why were they deflecting? "Will you tell me what the Rebel Gods are? If that woman is after us, I need to know what they are."

"That's very advanced for a trainee," Jude said.

"I just fought her and ended the curse. I deserve to know."

"Agreed," Ana said.

"Let us speak amongst ourselves," Jude said. "Then we will tell you."

Frustration boiled in my chest. This was *important*. I was tied up in it—I knew I was.

But Jude was already standing and shuffling us out of the room. Her face was stony. Protocol took precedence here, and Jude was nothing if not good at protocol. Even Caro, Ali, and Haris were booted.

A few moments later, we all stood out in the hall, the door shut in our faces. Jude, Hedy, and Cade remained within.

"Well, that's crap," Ana said.

"Rules are rules," Caro said. "Still, it's freaking annoying."

Tension thrummed under my skin. I shook my head. "Something big is happening." I looked at Ana. "Let's go find Arach."

Caro laughed. "You can't just go find Arach."

"I can go to her room and yell until she shows up."

"You might be yelling a long time," Ali said.

"I'm still going to try. I want answers. This has to do with me." I gestured between Ana and me. "With us. I want to know what it is."

And I needed to ask her why people had called me Njord, Rán, and Eir.

I turned away from my friends, hurrying down the hall toward the room Arach had appeared in when I'd first arrived here. Ana rushed to catch up, but Caro, Ali, and Haris stayed behind.

"Do you really think this will work?" Ana whispered.

"I don't know. I hope so." I found Arach's room a moment later. It was empty without that strong feeling of her magic.

I flicked on the light and entered the high-ceilinged room. Books lined the walls, and the quiet was thick.

"Arach!" I shouted.

Ana winced, covering her ears.

"Arach!"

Nothing.

"Arach, the Rebel Gods want me for something, and I want to

know what the heck they are. And people have been calling me by the names of Norse gods."

Magic shimmered on the air, just a hint of it. Then it hit me like a ton of bricks, right on the head. I wobbled.

Arach appeared a moment later, as ethereal as ever, her form somewhat transparent and her features almost human.

"The Rebel Gods, you say?" She drifted toward her chair but didn't sit. Instead, she peered at me. "Where did you hear of these Rebel Gods?"

"They sent a crazy jerk after me. Attacked the Protectorate with a dark curse meant to destroy the castle itself." I told her everything that had happened in the last two days.

She listened intently, her gaze never leaving my face.

"Don't forget the part about how people have been calling you by different names," Ana said.

Arach's gaze sharpened. "The Norse gods you mentioned?"

"A Venetian water creature called me Njord. So did Melusina in The Vaults. And then the Daughters of Rán said they reminded me of their mother. And finally, an old man called me Eir. They're all Norse gods. But I'm not a god."

Arach swayed on her feet, then sat in her chair. It was more of a controlled collapse, really.

I rushed forward. "What is it?"

"This man. Was he a healer?" Her voice sounded distant.

"Um, yeah. His grandson called him a healer." My heart raced. "What is it? What does it mean?"

Her gaze turned to me, surprised. Awed, even.

"You, Bree Blackwood, are a DragonGod."

"A *what?*"

Arach nodded, a smile spreading across her face. "We thought the last ones had been killed. You were supposed to be a myth. There could be no more. Yet you are here." Her gaze turned to Ana. "And you, too."

I sat hard in the chair across from her. "What is a DragonGod?"

That sounded really fancy. Really powerful.

Really *not me.*

"I don't feel like a DragonGod," Ana said.

"You will."

"But *what* are DragonGods?" I demanded.

"They are the magical children of the gods and the dragons. Long ago, the dragons and the ancient gods came together to create a new species so that the ancient powers could live on."

"What ancient powers?" My mind was whirring.

"For the most part, the gods no longer walk the earth. In rare cases, there are people like Cade. Earth-walking gods. But like I said, they are rare. One every few centuries. But the gods knew they could do great good in the world if only they were there. But since they could not be—because humans had stopped believing in them—they passed some of their powers on to worthy individuals. Like you."

"How, though?" I was so not buying this.

"That's where the dragons helped. We held on to their magic, gifting it to a worthy soul when they were born. We thought we'd gifted all the magic, but you're here. A dragon must have sensed you when you were born and given you your power."

"Why us?" Ana's voice was incredulous.

I couldn't blame her. My head was reeling.

"You are worthy. Your goodness and strength and determination." She looked at me. "And you, Bree—if you are being called Njord, Rán, and Eir… That means that you are the last Valkyrie."

"Weren't they the ones who chose the slain men from the battlefield to go to Valhalla?" I shook my head. "I really don't want to do that."

Arach smiled. "Yes. That was once their job. Like the gods, the Valkyrie no longer walk the earth. But you are a modern manifestation of them—the DragonGod who is powered by the magical gifts of the ancient Viking gods."

I blew out a breath. "I think you have this wrong. That can't be me."

I was a disaster. I was not the modern manifestation of a Valkyrie, imbued with the powers of dragons and the ancient Viking gods. The idea was ludicrous.

"It's you." Arach nodded. "And you'll slowly gain the powers of the Norse gods. Not all of their powers, but many of them volunteered little bits of their gifts to go to you. Have you heard voices when your power has come alive?"

Memories flashed. I sucked in a ragged breath. "Yes."

Arach nodded and smiled. "That's it, then. You are the Valkyrie of the DragonGods."

"Whew." Ana smacked the table. "That sounds cool."

Yeah, it kinda did. But was I ready for this?

"It's not all fun and games," Arach said. "Bree must learn to master her power. She must learn to make it rest easy inside of her, or she will be destroyed. Just like I said would happen with an Unknown."

"Is that why my sonic boom power disappeared?"

Arach nodded. "Most likely, yes. The powers will try to overtake each other. The sonic boom was not a gift from the gods, so it died first. You must work hard to make sure your magic is in harmony, or you will lose it all."

No. Losing your magic was like losing your soul. It'd leave me hollow and lifeless—unwilling to even live. It was a Magica's greatest fear. I swallowed hard. "How?"

"I am not sure," Arach said. "But we will find a way. We have resources to help you. A seer who may be able to provide guidance."

I hoped she was right. Because losing my magic... My soul...

I couldn't bear the thought. It made me cold just to think of it.

EPILOGUE

The next night, after a long day spent repairing some of the damage caused by the curse, we gathered at Whisky and Warlock to celebrate our victory. The place was full of Protectorate members, but our group had snagged the coveted corner table in our usual room. Sophie was keeping us plied with drinks, and some kind of Celtic rock played on the radio.

It was a good night. A great night.

After all the danger we'd faced, it was the *best* night.

"To Bree!" Caro raised a glass full of golden liquid and grinned.

"Who saved our arses!" Ali added.

I clinked my Cosmo with theirs, then tapped mine against Haris's and Ana's.

"Good, right?" Caro asked.

"Yeah. Fruity."

"That's the taste of victory," Ali said.

"Fruity?" I laughed.

"Victory tastes like security, in this case," Haris said.

"Which isn't a taste." Ali pointed at him, brows raised.

"She gets what I mean." Haris nodded at me. "Bree saved our

arses. That curse could have taken out the Protectorate. But it didn't—because Bree stopped it."

My cheeks heated, so I sipped to hide them. "I had a lot of help."

"Maybe," Caro said. "But you led the charge. I really do think you will have your pick of departments when your training is through."

"Pick the PITs!" Ali said. "We really are the best department. The Demon Trackers Unit does have some fun, but the PITs always get the best mysteries."

"And the prestige." Haris brushed some imaginary dust off his shoulder and put on a fancy accent. "Everyone is *very* impressed by us."

Caro laughed and punched him in the shoulder. "You know that's not true." She turned to look at me. "But I do hope you'll join us. You can do some real good with the investigative unit. You proved that with the dark curse."

"Thanks." I smiled, my chest warming with the knowledge that I had such good friends. "But it'll be a while before I cross that bridge."

I had to get my powers under control first, and figure out what it truly meant to be a DragonGod. I had to make my powers rest easy inside me so that they didn't devour each other....or my soul.

And we weren't done hunting the Rebel Gods woman. Worse, she wasn't done hunting us.

Ana caught my eye and smiled. But the same heavy knowledge darkened her eyes. The woman had proven she was powerful enough—and smart enough—to get to us. Just because we'd stopped her this time it didn't mean she wouldn't find another way.

We had to bring the fight to her. Somehow.

Ana squeezed my hand. "We've got this."

I nodded. There was a lot of *this*. But she was right. Together, we'd manage.

But tonight, we'd celebrate.

The drinks and conversation flowed, along with a rousing game of darts and the pub cat sticking its head into my chocolate martini to steal a sip.

Life was good.

Tonight was great.

But I couldn't help but occasionally peek around the pub for a sight of Cade. From what I could tell, he hadn't shown up, even though the whole Protectorate had come out. The pub was made of multiple rooms and corridors, some big, some small. All built at different times over the years. He might be in one of the other rooms—though this one was our usual preferred hangout.

If he were looking for me, he'd certainly come here.

I shook away the thought. As much as he'd driven me to distraction, he was right. It wasn't professional to be lusting after a colleague.

I played another round of darts, finally scraping a victory by a few points.

"Good job!" Ana high-fived me.

"I'll get you next time," Haris said.

"Yeah, you probably will." I grinned. "I'll be right back."

I turned and headed for the ladies' room. It was located in the far back corner of the pub, past the front door and through other small rooms. The place was like a maze.

Fortunately, there was no line for the toilet, as the hour was getting late. The other rooms of the pub weren't as full, either. When I passed by the entrance on my return to my friends, the door swung open.

Cade stepped inside, and I bumped into him. His strong hands came up, gently gripping my arms to steady me.

My heart leapt, my breath coming short.

Sparks jumped between us.

"Hey." I looked up, taking in his windswept hair and handsome face. He wore a long, dark coat that looked finely cut and somehow managed to make him look dangerous. Like he could take out a demon without breaking a sweat.

"Hi." A strange expression crossed his face, something I couldn't quite process. "Can I speak to you?"

I nodded, still surprised to see him. I'd given up on him showing.

He pulled me into a little snug room on the emptier side of the pub. A wide, wooden bench and table were crammed inside, but we found a nook in the corner that was hidden from the eyes of the other patrons.

I ended up with my back against the wall and Cade looming in front of me. His gaze was bright, his face torn. Tension thrummed between us, a desire so strong that it filled the air.

How the hell were we supposed to fake being normal?

"I tried to stay away, but I couldn't." Cade's voice was rough. "I don't want to pretend any longer."

Joy and confusion flashed through me. "What do you mean?"

"I like you, Bree. I thought I could ignore it. I can't. "

My heart raced. His gaze was riveted to my lips. Every inch of my body tingled. His storm-at-sea scent wrapped around me, clouding my mind.

"I can't, either," I whispered.

Kiss me. I begged with my eyes.

His big hands gripped my waist and pulled me toward him. My front pressed against his hard chest and I gasped, right before his mouth slanted against mine.

His lips were warm and skilled. I parted mine eagerly, plunging my hands into his hair and holding him tight to me. He kissed like a man possessed...like he couldn't get enough of me. As if he were going to die tomorrow and this was his last chance.

I was no better, my restraint stolen by desire. Heat blazed through me as his hands ran up my back, strong and broad. They felt like they covered every inch of me, making me imagine what else he could do with those hands.

I gasped and pulled back, startled by my own desire. My own greed for him.

He lifted his head, his breath coming short. His expression was pained, as if he couldn't bear to let me go. "You're right. Not here."

I nodded my head. "Right. Right." I swallowed hard. "I like to take it slow anyway."

"Normally, so do I."

I pressed a hand to his chest, trying to catch my breath. "Well, hold your horses, because I might *want* to jump your bones, but I'm not going to. Not yet. Not until I'm ready."

"Aye." He smiled, looking perfectly content with that. Though still a bit tortured.

"You're right, though. We can't pretend anymore. I'm ridiculously distracted by you. It's embarrassing."

"Likewise."

"What about the Protectorate?"

"It's not technically against the rules. It's more my own rule. It's dangerous to be distracted by the one you're working with. But I realized I'm going to be distracted by you no matter what."

"More so," I said. "Because we don't know what we're missing. All I do is wonder what kissing you would be like."

"Exactly. Even after I kiss you once, I want to know what the next time will be like."

"So, we'll just get it out of our system," I said. "Just like you said back in the stairway to the armorer's."

"That didn't work."

"Eventually, it will. We'll just let this run its course, and in a few weeks, we'll be back to normal. Colleagues."

Somehow, I doubted it. But it was the only thing I could think to say. I *did* want more with Cade—whatever that would turn out to be. But I wasn't willing to say, "Hey, let's be in a relationship."

We weren't even close to that point yet.

But some kissing and not pretending to ignore each other?

That would be great.

And if I could figure out what the Rebels Gods were, and how to get my power under control, I might live long enough to enjoy it.

THANK YOU FOR READING!

I hope you enjoyed Bree's first book as much as I enjoyed writing it. Reviews are *so* helpful to authors. If you want to leave one, you can do so on Amazon or GoodReads.

Join my mailing list at www.linseyhall.com/subscribe to stay updated. You'll also get a free ebook copy of *Hidden Magic*, the story of the FireSouls' early adventures. Turn the page for an excerpt of *Hidden Magic*. The story stars Cass, the girl that Bree and Cade visited in Magic's Bend.

EXCERPT OF HIDDEN MAGIC

Jungle, Southeast Asia
   Five years before the events in Ancient Magic

"How much are we being paid for this job again?" I glanced at the dudes filling the bar. It was a motley crowd of supernaturals, many of whom looked shifty as hell.

"Not nearly enough for one as dangerous as this." Del frowned at the man across the bar, who was giving her his best sexy face. There was a lot of eyebrow movement happening. "Is he having a seizure?"

"Looks like it." Nix grinned. "Though I gotta say, I wasn't expecting this. We're basically in a tree, for magic's sake. In the middle of the jungle! Where are all these dudes coming from?"

"According to my info, there's a mining operation near here. Though I'd say we're more *under* a tree than *in* a tree."

"I'm with Cass," Del said. "Under, not in."

"Fair enough," Nix said.

We were deep in Southeast Asia, in a bar that had long ago been reclaimed by the jungle. A massive fig tree had grown over and around the ancient building, its huge roots strangling the stone walls. It was straight out of a fairy tale.

Monks had once lived here, but a few supernaturals of indeterminate species had gotten ahold of it and turned it into a watering hole for the local supernaturals. We were meeting our contact here, but he was late.

"Hey, pretty lady." A smarmy voice sounded from my left. "What are you?"

I turned to face the guy who was giving me the up and down, his gaze roving from my tank top to my shorts. He wasn't Clarence, our local contact. And if he meant "what kind of supernatural are you?" I sure as hell wouldn't be answering. That could get me killed.

"Not interested is what I am," I said.

"Aww, that's no way to treat a guy." He grabbed my hip, rubbed his thumb up and down.

I smacked his hand away, tempted to throat-punch him. It was my favorite move, but I didn't want to start a fight before Clarence got here. Didn't want to piss off our boss.

The man raised his hands. "Hey, hey. No need to get feisty. You three sisters?"

I glanced at Nix and Del, at their dark hair that was so different from my red. We were all about twenty, but we looked nothing alike. And while we might call ourselves sisters—*deirfiúr* in our native Irish—this idiot didn't know that.

"Go away." I had no patience for dirt bags who touched me without asking. "Run along and flirt with your hand, because that's all the action you'll be getting tonight."

His face turned a mottled red, and he raised a fist. His magic welled, the scent of rotten fruit overwhelming.

He thought he was going to smack me? Or use his magic against me?

Ha.

I lashed out, punching him in the throat. His eyes bulged and he gagged. I kneed him in the crotch, grinning when he keeled over.

"Hey!" A burly man with a beard lunged for us, his buddy beside him following. "That's no way—"

"To treat a guy?" I finished for him as I kicked out at him. My tall, heavy boots collided with his chest, sending him flying backward. I never used my magic—didn't want to go to jail and didn't want to blow things up—but I sure as hell could fight.

His friend raised his hand and sent a blast of wind at us. It threw me backward, sending me skidding across the floor.

By the time I'd scrambled to my feet, a brawl had broken out in the bar. Fists flew left and right, with a bit of magic thrown in. Nothing bad enough to ruin the bar, like jets of flame, because no one wanted to destroy the only watering hole for a hundred miles, but enough that it lit up the air with varying magical signatures.

Nix conjured a baseball bat and swung it at a burly guy who charged her, while Del teleported behind a horned demon and smashed a chair over his head. I'd always been jealous of Del's ability to sneak up on people like that.

All in all, it was turning into a good evening. A fight between supernaturals was fun.

"Enough!" the bartender bellowed. "Or no more beer!"

The patrons quieted immediately. Fights might be fun, but they weren't worth losing beer over.

I glared at the jerk who'd started it. There was no way I'd take the blame, even though I'd thrown the first punch. He should have known better.

The bartender gave me a look and I shrugged, hiking a thumb at the jerk who'd touched me. "He shoulda kept his hands to himself."

"Fair enough," the bartender said.

I nodded and turned to find Nix and Del. They'd grabbed our

beers and were putting them on a table in the corner. I went to join them.

We were a team. Sisters by choice, ever since we'd woken in a field at fifteen with no memories other than those that said we were FireSouls on the run from someone who had hurt us. Who was hunting us.

Our biggest goal, even bigger than getting out from under our current boss's thumb, was to save enough money to buy conceal-ment charms that would hide us from the monster who hunted us. He was just a shadowy memory, but it was enough to keep us running.

"Where is Clarence, anyway?" I pulled my damp tank top away from my sweaty skin. The jungle was damned hot. We couldn't break into the temple until Clarence gave us the infor-mation we needed to get past the guard at the front. And we didn't need to spend too much longer in this bar.

Del glanced at her watch, her blue eyes flashing with annoy-ance. "He's twenty minutes late. Old Man Bastard said he should be here at eight."

Old Man Bastard—OMB for short—was our boss. His name said it all. Del, Nix, and I were FireSouls, the most despised species of supernatural because we could steal other magical being's powers if we killed them. We'd never done that, of course, but OMB didn't care. He'd figured out our secret when we were too young to hide it effectively and had been blackmailing us to work for him ever since.

It'd been four years of finding and stealing treasure on his behalf. Treasure hunting was our other talent, a gift from the dragon with whom legend said we shared a soul. No one had seen a dragon in centuries, so I wasn't sure if the legend was even true, but dragons were covetous, so it made sense they had a knack for finding treasure.

"What are we after again?" Nix asked.

"A pair of obsidian daggers," Del said. "Nice ones."

"And how much is this job worth?" Nix repeated my earlier question. Money was always on our minds. It was our only chance at buying our freedom, but OMB didn't pay us enough for it to be feasible anytime soon. We kept meticulous track of our earnings and saved like misers anyway.

"A thousand each."

"Damn, that's pathetic." I slouched back in my chair and stared up at the ceiling, too bummed about our crappy pay to even be impressed by the stonework and vines above my head.

"Hey, pretty ladies." The oily voice made my skin crawl. We just couldn't get a break in here. I looked up to see Clarence, our contact.

Clarence was a tall man, slender as a vine, and had the slicked back hair and pencil-thin mustache of a 1940s movie star. Unfortunately, it didn't work on him. Probably because his stare was like a lizard's. He was more Gomez Addams than Clark Gable. I'd bet anything that he liked working for OMB.

"Hey, Clarence," I said. "Pull up a seat and tell us how to get into the temple."

Clarence slid into a chair, his movement eerily snakelike. I shivered and scooted my chair away, bumping into Del. The scent of her magic flared, a clean hit of fresh laundry, as she no doubt suppressed her instinct to transport away from Clarence. If I had her gift of teleportation, I'd have to repress it as well.

"How about a drink first?" Clarence said.

Del growled, but Nix interjected, her voice almost nice. She had the most self control out of the three of us. "No can do, Clarence. You know... Mr. Oribis"—her voice tripped on the name, probably because she wanted to call him OMB—"wants the daggers soon. Maybe next time, though."

"Next time." Clarence shook his head like he didn't believe her. He might be a snake, but he was a clever one. His chest puffed up a bit. "You know I'm the only one who knows how to get into the temple. How to get into any of the places in this jungle."

"And we're so grateful you're meeting with us. Mr. Oribis is so grateful." Nix dug into her pocket and pulled out the crumpled envelope that contained Clarence's pay. We'd counted it and found—unsurprisingly—that it was more than ours combined, even though all he had to do was chat with us for two minutes. I'd wanted to scream when I'd seen it.

Clarence's gaze snapped to the money. "All right, all right."

Apparently his need to be flattered went out the window when cash was in front of his face. Couldn't blame him, though. I was the same way.

"So, what are we up against?" I asked.

The temple containing the daggers had been built by supernaturals over a thousand years ago. Like other temples of its kind, it was magically protected. Clarence's intel would save us a ton of time and damage to the temple if we could get around the enchantments rather than breaking through them.

"Dvarapala. A big one."

"A gatekeeper?" I'd seen one of the giant, stone monster statues at another temple before.

"Yep." He nodded slowly. "Impossible to get through. The temple's as big as the Titanic—hidden from humans, of course—but no one's been inside in centuries, they say."

Hidden from humans was a given. They had no idea supernaturals existed, and we wanted to keep it that way.

"So how'd you figure out the way in?" Del asked. "And why *haven't* you gone in? Bet there's lots of stuff you could fence in there. Temples are usually full of treasure."

"A bit of pertinent research told me how to get in. And I'd rather sell the entrance information and save my hide. It won't be easy to get past the booby traps in there."

Hide? Snakeskin, more like. Though he had a point. I didn't think he'd last long trying to get through a temple on his own.

"So? Spill it," I said, anxious to get going.

He leaned in, and the overpowering scent of cologne and sweat hit me. I grimaced, held my breath, then leaned forward to hear his whispers.

~

As soon as Clarence walked away, the communications charms around my neck vibrated. I jumped, then groaned. Only one person had access to this charm.

I shoved the small package Clarence had given me into my short's pocket and pressed my fingertips to the comms charm, igniting its magic.

"Hello, Mr. Oribis." I swallowed my bile at having to be polite.

"Girls," he grumbled.

Nix made a gagging face. We hated when he called us girls.

"Change of plans. You need to go to the temple tonight."

"What? But it's dark. We're going tomorrow." He never changed the plans on us. This was weird.

"I need the daggers sooner. Go tonight."

My mind raced. "The jungle is more dangerous in the dark. We'll do it if you pay us more."

"Twice the usual," Del said.

A tinny laugh echoed from the charm. "Pay *you* more? You're lucky I pay you at all."

I gritted my teeth and said, "But we've been working for you for four years without a raise."

"And you'll be working for me for four more years. And four after that. And four after that." Annoyance lurked in his tone. So did his low opinion of us.

Del's and Nix's brows crinkled in distress. We'd always suspected that OMB wasn't planning to let us buy our freedom, but he'd dangled that carrot in front of us. What he'd just said made that seem like a big fat lie, though. One we could add to the many others he'd told us.

An urge to rebel, to stand up to the bully who controlled our lives, seethed in my chest.

"No," I said. "You treat us like crap, and I'm sick of it. Pay us fairly."

"I treat you like *crap*, as you so eloquently put it, because that is exactly what you are. *FireSouls.*" He spit the last word, imbuing it with so much venom I thought it might poison me.

I flinched, frantically glancing around to see if anyone in the bar had heard what he'd called us. Fortunately, they were all distracted. That didn't stop my heart from thundering in my ears as rage replaced the fear. I opened my mouth to shout at him, but snapped it shut. I was too afraid of pissing him off.

"Get it by dawn," he barked. "Or I'm turning one of you in to the Order of the Magica. Prison will be the least of your worries. They might just execute you."

I gasped. "You wouldn't." Our government hunted and imprisoned—or destroyed—FireSouls.

"Oh, I would. And I'd enjoy it. The three of you have been more trouble than you're worth. You're getting cocky, thinking you have a say in things like this. Get the daggers by dawn, or one of you ends up in the hands of the Order."

My skin chilled, and the floor felt like it had dropped out from under me. He was serious.

"Fine." I bit off the end of the word, barely keeping my voice from shaking. "We'll do it tonight. Del will transport them to you as soon as we have them."

"Excellent." Satisfaction rang in his tone, and my skin crawled. "Don't disappoint me, or you know what will happen."

The magic in the charm died. He'd broken the connection.

I collapsed back against the chair. In times like these, I wished I had it in me to kill. Sure, I offed demons when they came at me on our jobs, but that was easy because they didn't actually die. Killing their earthly bodies just sent them back to their hell.

But I couldn't kill another supernatural. Not even OMB. It might get us out of this lifetime of servitude, but I didn't have it in me. And what if I failed? I was too afraid of his rage—and the consequences—if I didn't succeed.

"Shit, shit, shit." Nix's green eyes were stark in her pale face. "He means it."

"Yeah." Del's voice shook. "We need to get those daggers."

"Now," I said.

"I wish I could just conjure a forgery," Nix said. "I really don't want to go out into the jungle tonight. Getting past the Dvarapala in the dark will suck."

Nix was a conjurer, able to create almost anything using just her magic. Massive or complex things, like airplanes or guns, were outside of her ability, but a couple of daggers wouldn't be hard.

Trouble was, they were a magical artifact, enchanted with the ability to return to whoever had thrown them. Like boomerangs. Though Nix could conjure the daggers, we couldn't enchant them.

"We need to go. We only have six hours until dawn." I grabbed my short swords from the table and stood, shoving them into the holsters strapped to my back.

A hush descended over the crowded bar.

I stiffened, but the sound of the staticky TV in the corner made me relax. They weren't interested in me. Just the news, which was probably being routed through a dozen techno-witches to get this far into the jungle.

The grave voice of the female reporter echoed through the quiet bar. "The FireSoul was apprehended outside of his apartment in Magic's Bend, Oregon. He is currently in the custody of the Order of the Magica, and his trial is scheduled for tomorrow morning. My sources report that execution is possible."

I stifled a crazed laugh. Perfect timing. Just what we needed to hear after OMB's threat. A reminder of what would happen if he turned us into the Order of the Magica. The hush that had descended over the previously rowdy crowd—the kind of hush you get at the scene of a big accident—indicated what an interesting freaking topic this was. FireSouls were the bogeymen. *I* was the bogeyman, even though I didn't use my powers. But as long as no one found out, we were safe.

My gaze darted to Del and Nix. They nodded toward the door. It was definitely time to go.

As the newscaster turned her report toward something more boring and the crowd got rowdy again, we threaded our way between the tiny tables and chairs.

I shoved the heavy wooden door open and sucked in a breath of sticky jungle air, relieved to be out of the bar. Night creatures screeched, and moonlight filtered through the trees above. The jungle would be a nice place if it weren't full of things that wanted to kill us.

"We're never escaping him, are we?" Nix said softly.

"We will." Somehow. Someday. "Let's just deal with this for now."

We found our motorcycles, which were parked in the lot with a dozen other identical ones. They were hulking beasts with massive, all-terrain tires meant for the jungle floor. We'd done a lot of work in Southeast Asia this year, and these were our favored forms of transportation in this part of the world.

Del could transport us, but it was better if she saved her power. It wasn't infinite, though it did regenerate. But we'd learned a long time ago to save Del's power for our escape. Nothing worse than being trapped in a temple with pissed off guardians and a few tripped booby traps.

We'd scouted out the location of the temple earlier that day, so we knew where to go.

I swung my leg over Secretariat—I liked to name my vehicles

—and kicked the clutch. The engine roared to life. Nix and Del followed, and we peeled out of the lot, leaving the dingy yellow light of the bar behind.

Our headlights illuminated the dirt road as we sped through the night. Huge fig trees dotted the path on either side, their twisted trunks and roots forming an eerie corridor. Elephant-ear sized leaves swayed in the wind, a dark emerald that gleamed in the light.

Jungle animals howled, and enormous lightning bugs flitted along the path. They were too big to be regular bugs, so they were most likely some kind of fairy, but I wasn't going to stop to investigate. There were dangerous creatures in the jungle at night —one of the reasons we hadn't wanted to go now—and in our world, fairies could be considered dangerous.

Especially if you called them lightning bugs.

A roar sounded in the distance, echoing through the jungle and making the leaves rustle on either side as small animals scurried for safety.

The roar came again, only closer.

Then another, and another.

"Oh shit," I muttered. This was bad.

~~~

Join my mailing list at www.linseyhall.com/subscribe to get a free ebook copy of *Hidden Magic.*

AUTHOR'S NOTE

Thanks for reading *Academy of Magic!* Because the Fae world took up a large part of this book, there were fewer historical elements. However, the biggest one—The Vaults—are one of my favorites.

Edinburgh actually has several underground places, including the Vaults. They are also called the South Bridge Vaults and they are a series of chambers built in 1788 underneath the South Bridge in Edinburgh. Initially, they were used as workshops and taverns, but later they were a hotbed of criminal activity. As the vaults fell into disrepair, Edinburgh's poorest members of society moved in. B7 1860, they were in such terrible shape that they were empty. Mary Kings Close is another one of Edinburgh's underground districts. It is an alley that was closed off overtime until it was underground (and under buildings). It was occupied between the 16th and 19th centuries and in the 17th century was named for Mary King, the daughter of a wealthy advocate.

The Vaults as they appear in this book are a combination of these two places, set right under the castle in Edinburgh, which is located on a rock outcropping about three hundred meters high. The Grassmarket, the supernatural center of Edinburgh, is a real district in the Old Town (which, you guessed it, is the oldest part of Edinburgh). The Whisky and Warlock is located next to the current White Hart Inn, which is supposed to be the oldest pub in Edinburgh. But the Whisky and Warlock is based on an old Devon pub called the Lydford Inn. It's bigger, with more little rooms and snugs.

One thing you might have noticed in the book—all of the characters who called Bree by her godly names are species that share powers with that god. The Selkie, a seal who can turn into a human, called her by the name of the Njord, the god of water. The Daughters of Ægir called her Rán, who is a water goddess. And the healer in the Fae town called her Alateivia. In Bree, they recognized power like their own.

Well, I think that's it for the history and mythology in *Academy of Magic*. I hope you enjoyed the book and will come back for more of Bree, Ana, and Cade!

ACKNOWLEDGMENTS

Thank you, Ben, for everything. There would be no books without you.

Thank you to Lindsey Loucks, Adam at Fine Point Publishing, and Donna Rich for your excellent editing. The book is immensely better because of you! Thank you to Eleonora for your help with the Norse mythology.

Thank you to Orina Kafe for the beautiful cover art. Thank you to Collette Markwardt for allowing me to borrow the Pugs of Destruction, who are real dogs named Chaos, Havoc, and Ruckus. They were all adopted from rescue agencies.

GLOSSARY

Alpha Council - There are two governments that enforce law for supernaturals—the Alpha Council and the Order of the Magica. The Alpha Council governs all shifters. They work cooperatively with the Alpha Council when necessary—for example, when capturing FireSouls.

Blood Sorcerer - A type of Magica who can create magic using blood.

Dark Magic - The kind that is meant to harm. It's not necessarily bad, but it often is.

Demons - Often employed to do evil. They live in various hells but can be released upon the earth if you know how to get to them and then get them out. If they are killed on Earth, they are sent back to their hell.

Dragon Sense - A FireSoul's ability to find treasure. It is an internal sense that pulls them toward what they seek. It is easiest to find gold, but they can find anything or anyone that is valued by someone.

Djinn - Possesses invisibility and the ability to possess others for brief periods of time.

Earthwalking Gods - Reincarnates of the ancient gods who

can walk upon the earth. They are mortal but with all the power of that god.

Eclektica - A jack-of-all-trades who deals in spells.

Enchanted Artifacts – Artifacts can be imbued with magic that lasts after the death of the person who put the magic into the artifact (unlike a spell that has not been put into an artifact—these spells disappear after the Magica's death). But magic is not stable. After a period of time—hundreds or thousands of years depending on the circumstance—the magic will degrade. Eventually, it can go bad and cause many problems.

Fire Mage – A mage who can control fire.

FireSoul - A very rare type of Magica who shares a piece of the dragon's soul. They can locate treasure and steal the gifts (powers) of other supernaturals. With practice, they can manipulate the gifts they steal, becoming the strongest of that gift. They are despised and feared. If they are caught, they are thrown in the Prison of Magical Deviants.

The Great Peace - The most powerful piece of magic ever created. It hides magic from the eyes of humans.

Magica - Any supernatural who has the power to create magic —witches, sorcerers, mages. All are governed by the Order of the Magica.

Order of the Magica - There are two governments that enforce law for supernaturals—the Alpha Council and the Order of the Magica. The Order of the Magica govern all Magica. They work cooperatively with the Alpha Council when necessary—for example, when capturing FireSouls.

Seeker - A type of supernatural who can find things. FireSouls often pass off their dragon sense as Seeker power.

Seklie - Sea creatures lived off the coasts of Ireland and Scotland. They are seals who can also become human and draw their magic from the sea.

Shifter - A supernatural who can turn into an animal. All are governed by the Alpha Council.

Transporter - A type of supernatural who can travel anywhere. Their power is limited and must regenerate after each use.

Undercover Protectorate - A secret organization dedicated to protecting supernaturals and solving the crimes that no one else will.

Vampire - Blood drinking supernaturals with great strength and speed who live in a separate realm.

ABOUT LINSEY

Before becoming a writer, Linsey Hall was a nautical archaeologist who studied shipwrecks from Hawaii and the Yukon to the UK and the Mediterranean. She credits fantasy and historical romances with her love of history and her career as an archaeologist. After a decade of tromping around the globe in search of old bits of stuff that people left lying about, she settled down and started penning her own romance novels. Her Dragon's Gift series draws upon her love of history and the paranormal elements that she can't help but include.

COPYRIGHT

Copyright 2017 by Linsey Hall
Published by Bonnie Doon Press LLC

Linsey@LinseyHall.com
www.LinseyHall.com
https://www.facebook.com/LinseyHallAuthor
ISBN 978-1-942085-12-6